THE DARCKMOOR DEMON AND OTHER ENIGMAS

Who or what is responsible for the eerie howling from the night-darkened fells that disturbs the inhabitants of Darckmoor? Is there malice at work in the world of small presses? Why is there an eight-foot-high toadstool on the back of a truck speeding along a remote byway? When a new statue by a reclusive artist is displayed in a small gallery in London's East End, is it the beginning of something bigger? And what is the cause of the sorrowful single-mindedness of the long-term resident of an old-fashioned hotel?

JOHN LIGHT

THE
DARCKMOOR DEMON
AND OTHER ENIGMAS

Complete and Unabridged

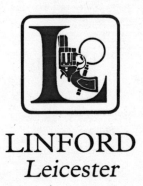

LINFORD
Leicester

First published in Great Britain

First Linford Edition
published 2014

*A catalogue record for this book is available
from the British Library.*

9|14

ISBN 978–1–4448–2123–9

Published by
F. A. Thorpe (Publishing)
Anstey, Leicestershire

Set by Words & Graphics Ltd.
Anstey, Leicestershire
Printed and bound in Great Britain by
T. J. International Ltd., Padstow, Cornwall

This book is printed on acid-free paper

Contents

The Darckmoor Demon

It was a cosy enough pub with a bright fire burning in the bar. Hugo and I sat in arm chairs on either side of the hearth. As usual when I'm in the north I was drinking Newcastle brown ale while Hugo quaffed John Smith's. A companionable silence had cocooned the room. There were only three other customers and each was a quiet drinker. The landlord perched on a stool behind the bar counter, his chin cradled by his hands, his eyes seemingly held by the fire. The radio on a shelf was not switched on and there was no sign of a television. The faint ululation of the wind outside emphasised the calm within. It was the epitome of civilised comfort. A log fell and sparks wafted up the chimney as the fire glowed hotter.

I had fallen into a pleasantly relaxed state, neither Hugo nor I feeling need of conversation anymore than the other occupants did. I think I may even have been half-dozing, certainly my mind was free-wheeling.

I was abruptly wrenched back to full consciousness of my surroundings by what I at first thought was a sudden surge in the noise of the wind. But as the sound increased in volume it changed its character, rising in pitch to a hideous shrillness and warbling in a hair-raising fashion that was entirely unlike any meteorological phenomenon I'd ever come across. Hugo was now staring at me, a slightly sardonic smile on his face.

'What the hell is that?' I whispered. He didn't answer immediately. The wail rose to a scream before abruptly diving to a deep base growl, rose again and then faded away altogether.

'Intriguing isn't it,' said Hugo. 'Suggest anything to you?'

'The hound of the Baskervilles?' I offered facetiously. 'Relocated from Dartmoor to Darckmoor?'

Hugo chuckled although it sounded to me more like a morale boosting laugh than genuine merriment.

'The lesson of Conan Doyle's story is

that there's always a rational explanation, even for the most outlandish sounds.'

'And the explanation for this blood-curdling noise?'

'I don't know,' admitted Hugo, 'but not, I fancy, a giant hound.'

Our fellow drinkers had not stirred and the landlord had exhibited no reaction.

'From the demeanour of our companions I deduce that it is well known to them at any rate,' I remarked with attempted light-heartedness.

Hugo stirred.

'I have talked to people around here about it. It is something they have grown used to without having any notion of what produces it, except that there's no special reason to believe it dangerous! It seems to have begun about five years or so ago.'

Our conversation was interrupted by the return of the unearthly howl. When it once more subsided, Hugo resumed.

'Not surprisingly, people here have come to refer to it as the Darckmoor Demon, recalling old legends.'

This was the first inkling I had that

Hugo had a deeper purpose in proposing this latest excursion to Northumberland.

I put it to him bluntly.

'Is that sound the reason you wanted me to join you in this outpost of the civilised world?'

'It does seem a bit like the end of the world here doesn't it. But look at this,' he said, as he handed me one of those half-size exercise books used in infant schools — roughly A5 landscape in size. It was filled, as anticipated, with childish print in pencil, the letters well-formed and easy to read. The thin book had slips of paper protruding from the top as markers. I naturally opened it at the first of these.

'my granddad is the devil,' I read, in a childish fist. In an adult hand, no doubt that of the teacher, the initial m, g, and d had been ringed and the appropriate capital printed above them. I turned to the next strip and on the page marked, I read, 'Granddad went Howling again in the Night.' Predictably the teacher had ringed the H and the N and written in the lower case letters. I turned the page to find: 'I was in bed. I herd grandad howling on the hill' The next marker was a few pages on. I glanced at the intervening pages — they seemed quite ordinary: 'I had bens and sosaj for te. I played with Toms dog. He gards the sheep.' 'gard' had been corrected, but on the next page it said 'I got a new car for my colekshun' and the teacher hadn't even attempted to alter the last word. The final page had 'Mum said its me or the old devil.'

I handed the book back to Hugo.

'It's a child's news book from year two,' he said, 'of a primary school in Alnwick. It was sent to me by his teacher who was a student of mine some years ago. Not surprisingly she's a bit worried about the boy who wrote that. She's asked him, as casually as she can, about what he writes but his answers have just confused and alarmed her further she says. She's reluctant to involve the education department's child psychologists in case it's just childish nonsense but gets blown up out of proportion and results in one of those terrible disruptions of a family we quite often read about in the newspapers. On the other hand it would be even worse if the lad really does need help and his need is just ignored. Rather as a last resort she asked me if I could give her any advice.'

Characterising himself as a last resort was so unlike Hugo that I decided he felt an unusual sense of involvement for some reason. As far as I knew, Hugo had no more contact with young children than I did — we both only interacted with them when they were eighteen or more and had three A levels. If Helen had lived I might by now have had children but fate determined otherwise.

'I don't know much about families really,' I ventured tentatively, 'but it looks as though the boy's granddad is living with them and getting on the mother's nerves — quite a common occurrence I would think. Calling someone an old devil is fairly common usage but might conceivably be taken literally by a child. Just from the evidence of the book itself I wouldn't imagine anything sinister. But the teacher knows the boy. She's in a much better position to judge than you or

I. In any case I don't see what you can do or how you can even give sensible advice.'

'Did you notice the boy's name? It was on the front of the book.'

I shook my head.

'It was Terence Darckmoor,' said Hugo. 'I know his father, Professor Roland Darckmoor.'

I instantly understood something of Hugo's interest in the matter and why he didn't just treat it with his usual academic detachment. Another thought struck me.

'Does the family have a connection with Darckmoor Fell? It surely can't be coincidence that they have the same name. Nor,' I went on accusingly, 'that we are now in the village of Underdarckmoor in close proximity to the fell itself.'

'No,' admitted Hugo. 'Roland is not exactly a close colleague; he is an anthropologist, but his speciality is evolutionary anthropology He made his name early on in East Africa. More recently, following his appointment to a chair at Sunderland, his interests have centred on the settlement of the British

7

Isles following the effective end of the last Ice Age some 10,000 years ago. Very little is known about the culture of the pre-Celtic peoples who moved in from the Ice Age refuges on the continent of Europe. Anyway, I know him well enough to be concerned.'

'You mean well enough to have an excuse for enquiring into young Terence's cryptic diary entries.'

'Perhaps so,' agreed Hugo.

'And old Mr Darckmoor?'

'I've never met any other members of the family. Roland's father is or was I believe some variety of farmer, sheep I think.'

After a comfortable night at the inn Hugo drove us back to Alnwick where we consulted the reference section of Alnwick library (these events occurred in the years immediately preceding the era of ubiquity of internet portals) but couldn't find what he wanted.

'Let's try Barter Books,' he said, 'they have an eclectic stock of old books as well as a wide range of modern titles. There just might be something there.' We walked the length of the town's main street to the former railway station which was now almost entirely occupied by one of the largest second-hand bookshops in the country. We poured ourselves coffee and sat in front of one of the coal fires which burned despite it being officially summer for it was a drear dreich day and we felt a need to dry the damp out of ourselves.

Feeling more comfortable, we began searching the shelves loaded with local history books, for references to Darckmoor. Eventually, Hugo found what he sought.

'Listen,' he said and read it out in a low voice. ''The oldest form of the name recorded is the polyglot *Dartmuir*, from the Celtic *dart*, meaning dark and the Scots *muir*, a variant of moor, but the meaning may reveal an older, pre-Celtic language tradition. In any case *Dartmuir* was gradually displaced by *Darkmoor* until in the nineteenth century the head of a local family with social pretensions persuaded cartographers of the Ordnance Survey to spell it *Darckmoor* to support his own spelling of his family's name as *D'Arckmoor*, a vain, in both senses of the word, pretence to Norman ancestry. His own descendants sensibly abandoned the apostrophe but the inserted and superfluous *c* persisted and may now be considered fixed.''

We had a healthy lunch in that singular bookshop, seated in what had once been the buffet of the rather grand (for a small town) terminus of the branch line from the junction at Alnmouth with the main London to Edinburgh Great North-Eastern Railway. Satisfied, we set off on the return journey to the village of Underdarckmoor. It was a lovely afternoon and Hugo chose a rather roundabout route taking the Rothbury road out of Alnwick across the moors past the leaning battlemented tower and barmkin wall of 14th century Edlingham Castle and then turning back north along the Vale of Glendale before once more heading west into the Cheviots.

Instead of stopping at the inn Hugo took the lane out of the village, further up the valley of the Darckwater. He drove unusually slowly, his eyes studying the terrain (instead of the road!). It was undeniably grim under the now overcast sky despite it being summer. The fell sides rose steeply on either hand and the skylines were crowned with crags of sandstone. At intervals the narrow way widened slightly to provide passing places and these were signed with tall metal poles that doubled as indicators of snow depth in winter. We seemed to be heading into a dead end when abruptly the road turned a hairpin bend and began climbing sharply up the hillside. Another hairpin in the reverse direction took us behind a fold in the land and hid the valley floor from us. We gained height rapidly, passing an impressive waterfall which Hugo said was Darckmoor Spout, until the upper valley of the Darckwater appeared in a shallower vale draining the higher fells.

Here there was a wide area of more level ground on which was built the grim bulk of Darckmoor House. The original peel tower was distinguished by the roughness of its stonework and absence of any windows wider than an arrow slit. A newer eighteenth century structure abutted and incorporated it, built in a provincial interpretation of the Georgian style.

'This place looks like the back of beyond,' I remarked.

Hugo gave a wry smile.

'The locals just call it 'Beyond' in fact. 'Don't go Beyond', is a local saying with deliberate ambiguity.'

The road ended in front of the building, widening in to an area big enough for several cars to park. Hugo pulled up next to a Landrover already there and we got out and approached the front door. Hugo knocked and it was opened without delay by a woman who looked surprised at seeing us.

'Forgive our unexpected arrival,' said Hugo with his most charming smile. 'I'm Hugo Lacklan and this is Alex Dunkley. I work in a similar field to Professor Darckmoor and as I was in this part of the world I hoped I might see him. I would have rung first but didn't have the number.'

'Why, yes I expect so. I'm his wife. Please come in and I'll tell him you are here.'

Mrs Darckmoor took me by surprise,

much younger than I reckoned her husband must be from what Hugo had recounted of his career. She had long blonde hair framing a pretty face, though one marked with strain. When she spoke her New Zealand accent was pleasant but tinged with the edginess which characterised her demeanour generally, something more I judged than our sudden arrival.

We waited in a wide passage and after a few minutes Roland Darckmoor appeared and one look confirmed my estimate of the relative ages of the two. He remembered Hugo and seemed perhaps more pleased to see him than professional shared interests might lead one to anticipate. The upshot was that, learning we planned to stay in the valley for a few more days, the Darckmoors insisted we move from the inn to their house so we duly drove back down to collect our luggage, such as it was. When we returned, Roland's father was also at home, having been out walking on the fell before. The family resemblance was clear. Roland and Elspeth Darckmoor's son Terence had also emerged from where ever he was before.

Elspeth Darckmoor announced that dinner would be ready soon and assured us there would be plenty for us too but she would show us our rooms first. I was pleasantly surprised by mine, which seemed to have been purged of the pervading gloominess of Darckmoor by her own sunny personality which I imagined would be her normal disposition rather than her current tension.

The conviviality of dinner was somewhat dimmed by the taciturnity of Mr Darckmoor. Inevitably, Hugo and Roland talked of anthropological subjects which left me, Elspeth and young Terence to entertain each other as best we might. Elspeth was a bright and knowledgeable conversationalist and I had taken an instant liking to the child, attractive in the way that almost all small children are before they begin that transmogrification to the almost infinite variety of unattractive adults. In addition he had his own personal traits which also exhibited a certain charm. He was observant, slightly solemn, maybe even a little withdrawn. If Helen had lived perhaps she and I could

14

have had a son like him. The thought filled me with a familiar melancholy.

After the meal, the elder Darckmoor left the table abruptly and a few minutes later the sound of the main outer door closing signalled that he had left the house.

'He usually goes for a walk after dinner,' was the only comment Roland Darckmoor made. The atmosphere seemed to lighten after the departure of Leonard Darckmoor. I offered to help Elspeth wash up and Hugo and Roland went to the latter's library to continue their discussion. Terence came with his mother and me to the kitchen where he sat at the table and read, while I washed the dishes and Elspeth dried and put away. A companionable silence settled on the room. When we'd finished Elspeth turned to the boy and said: 'Bedtime.' He made no protest but went up to his mother who bent down so he could whisper something in her ear. She straightened up and smiled at me.

'He asked if you'd read his story please,' she said, still smiling. I felt a glow of pleasure.

'Of course, I'd love to.'

'I'll come and tell you when he's ready.'

Terence was already in bed when I was summoned to his room. It was a comfortable size, with a ceiling sloping down towards the window which afforded a view of a hill crowned with a sparse stand of trees.

'I like your room,' I said.

'This is currently his favourite story,' said Elspeth, handing me a large book full of delightful pictures with a minimum of text.

'I hope I can do justice to it,' I said.

Although the words were few, they and the illustrations were perfectly matched and the story conveyed an air of sadness, perseverance and ultimate hope which was surprisingly affecting. My impression of this book, *The Flower*, stayed with me long after that reading, partly no doubt due to the circumstances which in retrospect seem to reflect the qualities conveyed by the book and I think I came to understand why it appealed to him so much at that time.

After we'd said goodnight to the boy

and Elspeth had tucked him in and kissed him, she and I were walking along the passage towards the stairs when she placed her hand on my arm and drew me to a halt.

'Thank you,' she said simply. 'You have a reassuring voice. He's been a bit tense lately and I could see him relaxing as you read. Do you have children of your own?'

'No,' I answered, feeling again that old yet recent sadness. 'My wife died before we'd got round to it. We imagined we had plenty of time but unhappily we were wrong.'

'I'm sorry,' she said. 'You would make a good father I am sure.' Then her voice changed.

'I realise I am imposing on you rather, but there's something I'd like your opinion on. It's in the study.' She led me to a small room with not much more than a desk, chair, cupboard, filing cabinet and shelves in it. On the wall was a drawing in a dark wood frame. At first I thought it was an abstract but then I realised that it was representational, but I was not clear of just what. It had a primitive and frightening air. Elspeth saw me looking at it. She gave an involuntary shudder.

'It's a drawing Roland did when he was a boy of a stone his grandfather kept on his mantel shelf. Roland said it used to frighten and fascinate him in about equal measure. He said he made lots of sketches of it and kept the one he thought best. After his granddad died the stone disappeared. I hate that picture! It gives me the creeps, but Roland won't get rid of it or even put it away. He says it's a reminder of an important time in his life.'

I could see why it made her uncomfortable. It had more than a suggestion of a pagan idol about it, with what looked like a hole going all the way through it and yet giving the impression of seeing. It had a definitely sinister aura about it. I smiled weakly.

'An early indication perhaps that he was going to be an anthropologist when he grew up,' I said.

Elspeth decisively turned her back on the image. From the cupboard she took a cardboard box which she opened to reveal a collection of loose photographs.

Shuffling through them she selected three and laid them side by side on the desk. It was obvious from the print styles that the right most one was the most recent and indeed was clearly Terence. I pointed to it.

'School photograph?' She nodded, her face relaxed in a happy smile.

The middle one was of a kind I recognised from my own schooldays and from the resemblance of the features to the first I guessed it was Roland and Elspeth confirmed that. The final one was of an earlier era still but the likeness to the others was marked if I ignored the clothes.

'Is that your father-in-law?' Again she nodded but this time her face was troubled.

'There's a strong family resemblance,' I ventured cautiously, wondering where the conversation was leading.

Elspeth replaced the photographs on top of the others and then reshuffled a hand-ful of them, before slipping her hand under the pile and extracting from beneath it an exercise book, one I judged to be from thirty or more years ago from its similarity to ones I remembered from my own child-hood. She thrust it towards me.

'Read it,' she implored, 'when you're on your own. Tell me what you think. Ask Hugo what he thinks if you like but don't let anyone else know you've got it.'

She opened the door and looked out into the passage. She listened.

'I think it's all clear. Take it to your room now.'

What could I do? Obeying her wishes seemed the only option. In any case Hugo had led me to believe that he and I were here to help in some undefined way and I sensed that this was connected to what-ever we were here to do.

Reaching my room I made myself comfortable in the armchair provided and opening the exercise book began to read.

I was always a little afraid of my grandfather. There was something in the way he looked at me which when I was very young, simply terrified me. Looking back the nearest I can get to describing it is a mixture of anticipa-tion, pity, and horror. I was glad when

I heard he was dead but old enough by then to feel ashamed of my relief. I was in fact just ten years old but it was not until I was much older that I learned the details of his death, what little there was to tell.

It seems my father had gone to visit the old man as he did from time to time. Sometimes he took me with him if I couldn't avoid it. I can still see in my mind the gloomy interior of the stone cottage, furnished in dark stained wood and heavy brown fabrics, more like a cave than a house. But this time he went alone. When he got there he found the door of the house ajar, he said. He pushed it open and went in. In the dim and over-furnished sitting room he found his father's corpse, his head against the hearth and disfigured with a large wound. The police gave evidence at the inquest that there were no finger prints in the house apart from my father's and grandfather's. There was no sign of a struggle nor of anything missing. There was no obvious weapon at the scene. The medical examiner stated that death was the result of a blow to the head which was in his opinion struck by a blunt instrument but he could not positively rule out accidental injury caused by the old man falling and bashing his head on the hearth There were no other injuries. The coroner said it was for the jury to decide whether the death was accidental or the result of foul play. The coroner's jury returned a verdict of murder by a person or persons unknown.

The police had virtually nothing to go on and made only a half-hearted attempt further to investigate the crime, if that was what it was. Of course they questioned my father closely because he had discovered the body and the police surgeon had testified that it had not been dead long. Nobody had seen anyone else go to the house but it was in a fold of the hill further up the fellside even than Darckmoor House and people kept themselves to themselves in those days and didn't like the authorities.

I do remember my father acting strangely at the time but he'd been *bereaved in a violent and shocking way so that didn't seem especially odd. What did seem strange and also frightening was that he began to look at me sometimes in the way the older man had done; but it was only occasionally and most of the time he was the dad I knew and loved.*

I assumed that the author of this odd and unsettling piece of prose was Roland judging by its appearance and Elspeth's actions, but whether it was intended as fact or fiction I couldn't decide. Nor could I decide what to say or do about it.

The next day was a strange one full of portent but of what I couldn't guess.

First thing in the morning, looking out of my window I could see the pre-sunrise sky — luminous pale orange clouds against a delicately blue empyrean — heart-breakingly beautiful but like all such beauty transient. As I watched, the clouds darkened and solidified in a fashion that my mood saw as ominous and I turned away to go down to breakfast.

Roland was still at the table and he told

me that Hugo was already up and out as was Mr Darckmoor. Elspeth had driven young Terence into Alnwick to school and was not yet back.

'I'm glad,' he said, 'to have this opportunity to speak to you alone. This may seem a bit odd.' He hesitated momentarily and then with an air of sudden determination, reached into his inside pocket and took out an envelope which looked as though it probably contained several sheets of paper, and held it out to me.

'I'd like you to look after this,' he went on, 'at least for a while.'

I looked at it. It was addressed to me but appended to my name was the alarming instruction: 'To be opened if anything serious befalls me — Roland Darckmoor.' I stared at him. He tried to make light of it but the implications made me very uneasy.

'I know we've only just met but I already feel I know you quite well.' He smiled. 'I've read your collection of short accounts of Hugo's enigmas and you've summed him up exactly! And whether you appreciate it or not, much of your own character is revealed in your writing.'

I was confused by this — I was in part flattered, but also puzzled by what he had said. However at this point Hugo returned and Roland stood up.

'I'm sorry,' he said, 'but I have some work I must do — deadlines!' He grimaced.

'Don't worry,' replied Hugo. 'The country round here looks interesting. We'll go for a walk.' He turned to me. 'Is that all right with you?'

'Fine,' I answered, concealing my slight irritation at his obvious assumption that it would be. However I had done Hugo an injustice for as soon as we were alone he apologised.

'Sorry to pre-empt your agreement but I feel there's some need for urgency. Can you be ready to go out in five minutes?' I nodded.

'I just have to get an anorak and knapsack and put my boots on.'

We were soon toiling up the fell-side and as we gained height more of the stand of pines came into view than had been visible from below until I could see that the trees whose tops could be glimpsed above the fold in the hill when viewed from the house were just the outliers of an extensive wood. Beyond its margins the deeper wood was more mixed but with a predominance of oaks, so gnarled and of such broad girth as to be evidently very old. Hugo angled slightly towards the west as though aiming to reach the edge of the trees at a particular place, and so it proved. When we reached them Hugo gestured.

'Look at this.' A group of stumps stood a little forward of the bulk of the trees, and an ill-defined corridor stretched away behind them through the wood northwards, where trees had been felled at some time perhaps as a rough firebreak. Hugo made no further comment but set off again along the trees' edge further westward still until we came to another feature similar in the pattern of the forward standing group, but here the work was clearly more recent. A number of firs had been felled but the timber had not yet been cleared away and still lay around a now isolated group of tall upright boles from which the twigs and branches had been stripped to leave them bare. I imagine the older group would have looked much like this before they were reduced to stumps.

'This, I fancy, is the explanation of the fiercesome sounding howling,' he remarked. 'Winds channelled through this strange arrangement of trunks might have produced the unearthly notes we heard.'

'Who would contrive such an effect and why?' I queried. Hugo shrugged, but there was a half-smile on his lips. He reached into his pocket and taking out a slim booklet, offered it to me. It had been written by an earlier Darckmoor sometime around 1850, and contained a number of theories concerning the howlings attributed to the 'Darckmoor Devil', including the idea that unusual tree arrangements might funnel the winds in just the right way to produce them.

'I found this in Roland's library,' he said. 'It made me wonder . . . '

A little further on we came to a rough path leading into the wood. Hugo led the way along it and as we penetrated deeper it grew gloomy. After perhaps half an hour we came to an outcrop of rock which loomed to the height of the trees surrounding it. I followed Hugo round the cliff until we came to a small cave. Hugo had come prepared for this with a torch, indeed it had been clear to me for some time that he had been this way earlier and had some idea of what to expect.

We ducked and entered the cave. It wasn't very large and we couldn't quite walk upright, but it was dry and like most caves maintained a comfortable temperature. At the entrance there were the ashes and charred branches of a fire, and a small pile of cigarette stubs. Indicating them, Hugo suggested this was probably where Leonard Darckmoor spent his evenings.

'Why not just a tramp?' I suggested. Hugo shook his head.

'Tramps or other indigents either smoke their cigarettes completely or save the butts to recover the unburnt tobacco and roll new ones.' I nodded at the overwhelming likelihood of this.

Towards the back of the cave Hugo shone the torch on an object leaning against the cave side. I stared at it; it had a stylised animal head with gaping mouth atop a tall apparently bronze tube. The full length of it must have been about twelve feet. It was certainly too long to have been stood upright in the cave.

'What on earth is it,' I whispered.

'It's a carnyx, an iron age war horn,' answered Hugo, 'or rather it's a reconstruction of one. The Celts used them in battle.'

'You don't think it's this rather than the tree formation that's responsible for that awful noise?'

Hugo was quite definite.

'No. Roland told me about this horn. He had it made as part of some work he's been doing; he's heard it played and he says it is nothing like the sound the demon is credited with. He brought it home with him from the University for safe-keeping and, ironically, it went missing. Clearly someone stole it and hid it here; my guess would be old Mr Darckmoor.'

'Shall we carry it back down?'

'No. Best leave things in place until we know what is significant.'

We walked further on until we cleared the edge of the wood and the fell stretched treeless away into the distance, it's barren appearance relieved only by gorse bushes here and there and swathes of low heather. The views seemed endless in all directions, Darckmoor House and the few cottages near it, miniaturised by distance. Eventually we came to a path leading down off the fell. Hugo consulted his map and said it should take us down to the Darckwater valley close to the inn where we'd stayed. When we got there we had a pre-prandial beer and then trudged up the lane to Darckmoor House.

'Elspeth rang to say she'd met some friends and was staying in Alnwick for lunch,' was Roland's greeting, 'but she told me what was in the larder and the fridge so we can feed ourselves. Or we could go down to the pub,' he grinned.

'What about your father?' I asked.

'Hm, yes, you're right. We'd better stay here in case he returns and wonders where everybody is.' There was ham and butter, cheese and home-baked bread. Accompanied by more beer it made a satisfying repast. Mr Darckmoor arrived before we'd finished and he joined us at the table. He seemed less taciturn than the previous day and Hugo encouraged him to tell us something of the area and how it had changed over his lifetime. After lunch, Hugo and I explored more of the fell but found nothing of further seeming significance. We returned mid-afternoon.

Elspeth arrived back with Terence later in the afternoon. She apologised for her day-long absence but it looked as though the brief respite from the dolorous environs of Darckmoor had done her good. She promised us a good meal for dinner to make up for our rustic lunch and was as good as her word. Nevertheless Leonard Darckmoor had relapsed into his normal moroseness.

As on the previous evening I helped wash up but the easy camaraderie of yesterday seemed to have evaporated. Once again I read Terence's bedtime story, the same one as before. When

Elspeth descended to the drawing room, Leonard had gone out again. The four of us decided to play bridge and as we were all of a similar competence it proved an absorbing series of rubbers, successfully taking our minds off the prevailing tensions in the house.

When we all finally retired, Hugo suggested that I remain fully awake and dressed. I struggled to stay alert after our strenuous day on the fell, but I was rudely shocked back to full awareness by the same unearthly howling I had heard two nights previously. Now that I knew what it was I expected to be unmoved by it but its uncanny power to disturb was hardly diminished and I was quite pleased when Hugo tapped on my door and joined me. As the howl finally died away it was supplanted by a harsher, even more sinister, sound. Hugo immediately started to his feet.

'Come on,' he hissed. 'No time to lose; but quietly.' We went out through the porch, pausing to shrug on our coats. Hugo set a fierce pace along the track that angled up the hillside through the mist. We retraced our footsteps of earlier in the day and once we were above the mist, a nearly full moon made following the way easier until we entered the wood where it was much more difficult.

We advanced into the cave with circumspection but it was empty — more so than earlier for the carnyx had gone. The moment I registered its absence I heard again the notes of strident provocation that had followed the usual howling and felt sure it was the carnyx we had heard. We hastened out of the cave in time to hear it boom again. It was hard to be sure of the sound's direction but we both turned towards the path leading upward through the trees to higher crags. I thought I heard a cry and Hugo increased his pace still further so that I was hard-pressed to keep up.

Abruptly a crag loomed above us and we scrambled as fast as we could up the least steep side to the summit. Reaching it we stood breathing heavily. The crag fell away on the west to bare hillside bereft of trees, a rock strewn, heather clad wilderness with only the stunted gorse to relieve its monotonous appearance, stark and grey in the moonlight.

On the highest point of the crag a dark shape seemed out of place. Hugo pulled out his torch and its light revealed the body of Roland Darckmoor. By his side was the war horn, broken in two, the carved animal head detached from the long bronze tube. Hugo checked Roland's pulse. He looked up and shook his head.

'Where's Leonard?' I wondered aloud. Again Hugo shook his head.

'He may have returned to the house without us seeing him. If he's still out here, with the darkness and that mist that's rising it's unlikely we can find him. A search would have to wait until the morning.'

'He may be injured,' I objected.

Hugo looked doubtful, nevertheless he did concede I might be right.

'We'll go straight back to the house,' he said, 'and if he isn't there we'll call the police. They'll know if it's practical to organise a search. In any case it would be best for Roland's body to be recovered as soon as possible.' It seemed to me that Hugo had been badly knocked off balance by events and wasn't thinking as clearly as normal.

'You go back,' I replied. 'I'll stay with Roland.' Perhaps I wasn't being all that rational either and should have seen that it would be safer for Hugo and I to stick together, but I felt it would be wrong to leave Roland unattended even though we were sure he was dead and it would be no more than keeping a vigil if I were to remain by his side. Nowadays of course, a call from a mobile telephone would have meant we could both remain and still raise the alarm, although we might not have been able to even now as coverage is patchy in these remote areas of high ground. Still it is difficult to recall how it was then, when even a short distance meant isolation and separation from the human herd.

Hugo was unhappy about my decision. 'Keep a keen look out,' he cautioned. 'Leonard could be somewhere out here and we've no idea what he's capable of.' I didn't find that reassuring, but it didn't undermine my resolve. Some deep primitive instinct moved me I suppose.

Hugo disappeared very quickly as he left

and I realised this was because the mist, cold and clammy, was rising still faster up the hillside and it rapidly enveloped me. With the curtailment of visibility I felt increasingly nervous at being alone and isolated on the fell with the body of a man whom I had to recognise might possibly have been murdered in which case his murderer was probably still on the loose so when a dark figure loomed out of the murk I almost gasped. I'd been crouched next to Roland as if affording and feeling some kind of companionship but now I straightened up.

Leonard Darckmoor stared at me seemingly without recognition. He shouted but I could make nothing of the sounds. If they were words with meaning they were in no language I recognised. Perhaps Hugo would have known. The elder Darckmoor raised his arm and shook his fist threateningly. In it he clasped what looked like a stone age axe. It was stained darkly. I shuddered. Not with his son's blood surely? Suddenly I was as fearful for Hugo's safety as my own. Could Hugo have encountered Leonard and himself fallen victim?

My thoughts returned immediately to myself — if Hugo was dead or injured no help would come to me; I'd have to seek it myself. I noticed that the gloom was deepening, whether from the thickening mist or cloud hardly seemed of consequence.

Abruptly Darckmoor seemed to calm down; his eyes focused and he appeared to recognise me. When he spoke it was in ordinary English with his customary soft Northumbrian accent.

'Is Roland dead?'

'Yes,' I replied. 'Hugo's gone to get help.'

'I grieve for my son, but it is for the best.'

I was unable to think of any adequate reply. I waited, hoping he would explain what he meant but as he didn't, I prompted him.

'Why do you say that?'

'Because of the demon I harbour.'

Then he raised his arm again and cursed — or at least that's what it sounded like but he had reverted to the incomprehensible strings of syllables and I could identify no words among his utterances. He stretched his arm to its fullest extent and at that moment the wind tore a rent in the mist through which the moon's baleful light gleamed. It fell on the stone and I saw it was the original of the one in Roland's childhood drawing. As Leonard moved his arm again, the moon's light shone directly through the hole in the stone, giving it the appearance of an eye in a skull, an eye not for seeing, but for projecting the soul and it was glaring straight at me!

Suddenly he let out a final blood-curdling howl and swung away from me and disappeared once more into the hill fog.

My vigil felt interminable at the time but in fact Hugo must have acted with commendable dispatch, and as the night dragged towards morning and the darkest hour which is proverbially always before the dawn, powerful torches at last pierced the gloom and I shouted out with relief to assist their final approach. Hugo was accompanied by the local doctor and a number of uniformed and plainclothes police and police dogs. I confess that I was so pleased to have company once more that I hardly gave poor Roland a thought as we picked our way carefully down towards Darckmoor

House, Roland's body carried on a stretcher by two policemen. I was abruptly recalled to a proper sense of the tragedy when we arrived and were confronted by a stricken Elspeth Darckmoor and her frightened son.

Two policemen remained with us at the house for what little remained of that ill-starred night in case Leonard Darckmoor returned but he did not. The next morning the mist cleared coincidentally with the arrival of another contingent of policemen and dogs and the search for Leonard Darckmoor was soon underway. He was eventually found, dead at the bottom of a crag from which he had fallen and broken his neck. Or perhaps he threw himself off it.

It was not until after the police had left that I recalled the letter which, with what now seemed commendable foresight, Darckmoor had left me.

Dear Dr Dunkley,

Although our acquaintance has regrettably been so short, I have rapidly grown to trust you, both your integrity and your judgement. I sense that Elspeth does too. I realise that what I am going to ask of you is no light matter, and for that I apologise, but I can think of no one more reliable. I had envisaged it would be Hugo I confided in but there is the possibility his professional instincts, (so similar to my own that I believe I have some insight into what motivates him!) may prevent him seeing what is best for my family.

Since you will only be reading this if something devastating has happened to me, that part at any rate will be clear, and my request is quite simply that you endeavour to shield my wife and son from the consequences of whatever has occurred. It may help you to understand events if you read the enclosed papers.

Counting on your acquiescence, I thank you in advance for whatever you are able to do to help my family.

Yours gratefully
Roland Darckmoor

The additional pages were firstly a draft of a paper on the simulation of the howling of a deity of the North Wind, a putative fore-runner of the Greek god Boreas. Roland had attached a note to the draft, not for publication but meant for me, in which he had scribbled: 'In an attempt to explain the stories of the Darckmoor Devil which were rife some 150 years ago, I was led to fashion the group of wind-howl generating trees, modelled on an earlier group fashioned apparently purposefully, although it might have occurred by unhappy accident. Unfortunately, the sounds they produced seemed to have a profoundly disturbing effect on my father.'

Secondly there was a report of DNA ancestral determinations from a reputable source, addressed to Leonard Darckmoor, and purportedly demonstrating a predominance of pre-Celtic genes in his make-up. A note clipped to this in what seemed to be Roland's hand commented:

From things he said it was clear that Dad had come to believe our ancestors had a prior claim to Albion over the Celts and felt a particular resentment towards the Celtic Goddodin who roamed the lands before they in turn were ousted by the Angles and the area received its present name Northumbria, and this had fostered an unreasoning prejudice against the Celts and all subsequent 'invaders' of the island. This would have been perhaps a harmless eccentricity in itself but it conspired with other things to veer towards madness.

My father told me that his father had told him that he was possessed by the personality of a remote ancestor which my father reasoned had travelled down the line of Y-chromosomes from remote antiquity, indeed from shortly after the repopulation of these islands following the last ice age some ten or twelve thousand years ago. We would hardly be unique in being descended from those distant and truly 'Ancient' Britons. The weight of DNA evidence is persuasive that the majority of modern Britons are indeed descended from such ancient Britons certainly through maternal lines. His father believed that when he himself died this ancestor would migrate to my father in some unspecified way. After my own son was born Dad became obsessed with the fear that the demon, as he called it, would migrate to me and thence to my son and so continue down the Darckmoor line. As each year passed he grew increasingly preoccupied by the urge to prevent this happening. On one occasion he even confided to me that the only way he could see of averting this would be for he and I to commit a joint suicide far away from young Terence. I tried to persuade him to seek medical advice but he had reached the stage where he simply became angry at any suggestion that his beliefs were a delusion.

My father gave an unusually (for him) eloquent and impassioned description of the moment of his father's death (without actually saying whether he had killed him himself, although that seemed to me the unavoidable conclusion) and insisted he experienced the monster leaping into and settling in his own mind. The prehistoric ancestor now dwells there as it had lived in all our forefathers' for *a thousand generations and still crouches there, compelling him to harbour it, enjoying life through him, waiting and watching until the time comes that he will trick me into murdering my father in turn and becoming the next vessel for the cacodemon.*

I now have a much greater appreciation of what people of earlier centuries meant when they talked of deranged unfortunates being possessed and I am becoming increasingly worried that Dad may attempt to bring about his joint suicide 'solution' to the threat he imagines.

After pondering only briefly I decided to show the letter and accompanying documents to Hugo and we did of course do as much as we could to smooth over the enquiries and expedite the formalities that necessarily followed the sudden demise of two generations of the Darckmoor family. Before we left Darckmoor we apprised Elspeth of the contents of Roland's letter to me, and left the documents with her. We returned of necessity for the inquests and Elspeth told us she was keeping the documents out of the public domain, and Hugo and I agreed not to mention them. To do so would invite malign gossip and they provided no new facts about the events, just speculation. In the end verdicts of accidental death were recorded on both men. The stained hand axe I had seen in Leonard Darckmoor's grasp had not been seen by anyone else. I presumed he'd dropped it in one of the border meres before he fell, in which case there was scarcely any chance whatsoever that it would come to light.

Hugo and I have since speculated about the exact sequence of events. Hugo inclines to the idea that Roland decided he must bring matters to a head in the hope of preventing an unpredictable deterioration in the situation and that it was he who had taken the carnyx from the cave to the crag and had sounded the notes that followed those produced by the wind, and that he had done it as a deliberate provocation to bring about a confrontation. He presumably thought he could control events but the old man had proved too strong for him, had hit him with the hand axe and then broken the war horn. He feels that it's probable Leonard then recovered most of his senses and deliberately threw himself from a crag, partly in remorse and partly to put paid to the demon, as he believed.

I prefer to be more charitable and assume that Leonard planned to commit suicide all alone and far from Roland with the same intention but unfortunately Roland caught up with him and tried to thwart him whereupon Leonard struck him with the axe but without expecting to kill him, but just so that he could put distance between them. I admit that doesn't explain the presence of the broken carnyx. We do agree however that if we had told the inquest all we actually knew or suspected and the coroner had reached similar conclusions to Hugo and so recorded verdicts of murder followed by suicide, we would have failed to honour Roland's plea that we should protect his family as far as we could.

Elspeth Darckmoor was a resolute woman

and despite her grief she found the internal strength to cope for her own and her son's sake and I found she needed little practical help, just occasional encouragement and reassurance that what she was doing was the best thing. She fairly quickly sold Darckmoor House and purchased a flat in Alnwick away from the horrors of recent events and within easy reach of Terry's school. Two years ago though, she returned to Auckland in her own country with their son.

I previously wrote under a pseudonym a short story based on the Darckmoor incidents, although using fictional characters and a quite different setting and, of course, not using the Darckmoor name. I even changed the action somewhat. In short I more or less completely fictionalised it, and with the title *Survivor* it was published in *Ballista* (a small press magazine of fantasy, science fiction and the supernatural which should indicate the extent of my fictionalisation) but not long ago I had a letter from Elspeth in which she said she's now told Terence about the family's history. She wrote that she judged he was old enough to handle it and it does indeed sound from her subsequent correspondence as though he has taken it in his stride.

She'd concentrated all the madness on the old man emphasizing the belief that she desperately wanted to make the truth, that it was personal to him, not hereditary as some of the circumstantial evidence might suggest. It was clear to me, perhaps reading more into the letter than she meant to reveal, that she hadn't entirely convinced herself, that her telling of Terence had been partly motivated by a need on her part to put him on his guard, warning him to be alert for any sign of mental malaise.

She'd keep her maternal eye on him as long as she could, of that I had no doubt, but that couldn't, indeed shouldn't, be for ever. She concluded her most recent letter by saying that she was grateful for mine and Hugo's long silence with respect to the happenings we'd shared but that if I wanted now to make fuller disclosure of the actual events she had no objection. She has remarried and sounds happy with her new husband and they have provided two half-siblings for Terence, in proof as it were of this.

So I feel it will do no harm to reveal the true facts of the matter to anyone who cares to read these pages. I have never been happy at dissimulation, and hope the truth may be of interest to students of Northumberland events and perhaps even of psychology, crime and aberrant behaviour generally.

The Enigma of
Poetic Injustice

I suppose it would be more attention grabbing to call this account something like *The Small Press Murders* but quite apart from this being ambiguous I find that kind of sensationalism distasteful. *The Enigma of Poetic Injustice* is of course vague well beyond the point of ambiguity but it has something of the air of a metaphysical painting by De Chirico about it that I find appealing.

Rereading my first draft of this account there seemed something odd about it and I suddenly realised why: it all happened in the early nineties before mobile phones and especially the internet became ubiquitous. Their advent has so completely changed the way we live that we now expect to know of everything almost as it happens! The old world of slow percolation of information seems inconceivable, but that really is the way it was such a very short time ago.

Unlike most of the enigmas which I have chronicled, this was one into which I was not dragged by Hugo Lacklan, but a case in which I interested him and it came to my attention because I was myself a participant in the world of the small presses.

If you imagine that this world is the preserve of ancient spinsters of limited means and sheltered lives free of the uglier emotions which disfigure the 'big' world, disabuse yourself! The age range is almost total and those involved if not exactly a cross section of society then certainly a very varied bunch. All human life is there, to redeploy a grubby slogan — deranged writers, mad editors, crusading critics and rabid reviewers; but at the other end of the spectrum there are fine writers, discerning editors, careful critics and learned reviewers, and a multitude of gradations between them. This habitat has its own dangers ranging from the risk of mildly hurt feelings occasioned by rejections to the extremes of bitter literary

51

feuds of extraordinary venom — though conducted at pens' length of course. And the adjective 'small' does many of the titles an injustice. Although some of them have very rough reproduction methods, mere stapled photocopied A4 pages of typed work, the production values of the more ambitious are equal if not superior to magazines and journals more widely known in the 'big press' world. Nor is quality of appearance an infallible guide to that of the poems contained. Poetry gold can be found in the meanest magazines and dross in the smartest, although the ambitions of individual poets and editors do tend to sort the magazines into a hierarchy of quality of production and talent.

This was the milieu into which I ventured in search of that mild euphoria of seeing my work in print and on occasion finding it mentioned favourably in reviews. I'm not sure what got me started writing poems. I think the death of my wife Helen had something to do with it and certainly the penning of these accounts of Hugo Lacklan's 'Enigmas' gave me the confidence to essay creative writing in general.

In time I became friends with editors and even a few other writers with whom I felt an affinity. They were strange two dimensional relationships reflecting the dimensionality of paper sheets, our medium of communication. I knew nothing about them that wasn't transmitted through their poetry and occasional letters. I knew their addresses but not what sort of lives they lived at them, I knew their names though not whether they were their real ones, not their ages nor even their sex since although reading their poems I gained impressions of both, those impressions may have been wildly in error. It was a comfortable largely undemanding inter-action.

Magazines appeared at most monthly but more generally quarterly, annually and some at longer or at irregular intervals. It is not a world for the eager or impatient so I assumed that its denizens were mostly past their first youth! Occasionally a brash, thrusting or earnestly eager maga-zine would erupt on the scene but such rarely continued for long, either disappearing or adapting to the more leisurely pace of the majority.

So it was seldom immediately obvious when a magazine eventually died. Sometimes an editor would announce in advance that they were ceasing publication but more generally it became apparent only with the return of a submission with a brief regretful note or when letters were returned undelivered and annotated 'gone away' or 'not at this address' or just disappeared without trace.

The demise of *Brill Poetry Quarterly* was different. Its title was not a slangy claim to excellence but was after the Buckinghamshire hamlet of that name. An extended silence had started me wondering if it had reached the end of its natural life and quietly expired when the stamped addressed envelope (s.a.e as it's abbreviated in the trade) enclosed with my latest submission arrived in my post. It contained as I expected my rejected poems but the covering letter was not at all what I anticipated. It was from the editor's sister, a Mrs Anderson. It was of course a form letter but it announced that sadly the editor Adele Simpson had died unexpectedly and that consequently *Brill Poetry Quarterly* would no longer be published. Mrs Anderson felt sure her sister would have wanted her to thank the contributors for their support over the years and wish them well for the future.

I was saddened by the letter, by its reminder of the mortality that haunts all our futures and perhaps most of all by the realisation that I had known so little of Adele Anderson that her death should come as so complete a surprise. Unlike the death of a magazine, the death of its editor has the human quality that affects us most personally.

The following Sunday afternoon I was at a bit of a loose end, unable to settle to work or writing, gardening or to tackling any of the dozen odd jobs that needed doing around the cottage in the Chiltern Hills where I lived at that time, and on an impulse I got the car out and drove up to Aylesbury. From there I took the A41, ancient Akeman Street, through Waddesdon to Kingswood where I turned off into the narrow lanes crisscrossing the Vale of Aylesbury. Passing through the village of Ludgershall I was soon climbing the short but steep incline to the hilltop crowned by the harnlet of Brill. I parked and set off for a stroll around. The few shops were shut, because it was Sunday afternoon I supposed, and I saw no people about. The tiny settlement seemed fast asleep in the warm sunshine. On one edge I found a post mill, its sails as still and silent as everything else in the place. Its position on the hill brow above the steep slope to the Vale would have given it a plentiful supply of wind to power the sails when it was working.

At the end of another of the short lanes leading off the main street, I found the cottage where Adele Anderson had lived, a picturesque dwelling on the opposite edge of the hill from the mill but with a similar wide and windy view, as immediately after the cottage this lane too plummeted down the hill. The situation accorded well with the ambience of the magazine she edited but seeing it told me nothing else about her.

That should really have been the end of the matter as far as I was concerned — a brief *memento mori* and then on with the motley! But then I had a letter from Eddie Thurrock. Unlike most denizens of the poetry demi-monde, he was one with whom I'd gradually formed a distant but enduring friendship. He mentioned his own surprise at Adele Simpson's death. He'd met her at some literary festival a while ago and said she was quite a lot younger than he was. (He himself was not old, I knew, as I'd seen in a magazine a photograph of him taken at a recent book launch). He also wrote that he knew of three other magazines that had closed recently following the demise of their editors, remarking that it seemed a lot. I thought so too although I couldn't do any sort of statistical analysis of the apparent cluster as I had no figure for the total number of magazines there might be. Not long afterwards he wrote to me again enclosing a newsletter put together by an enthusiast and printing various items of news from independent presses and which included some comments of its own on the passing of *Brill Poetry Quarterly* which coincided with Eddie's and mine: 'If I was older,' he'd written, 'I'd suspect it was just a question of having reached that time of life when one's acquaintances begin to thin out, but I happen to know none of these editors was that sort of age. It's almost enough to make me wonder if dark forces are at work — and I'm only half joking!'

Thus, ineluctably, was I drawn into the investigation of a series of unexpected deaths in that largely unobtrusive world of small independent publications devoted in the main to poetry. Inevitably I mentioned all this to Hugo next time he was in London and we found time for lunch together in an East End pub. He was as interested as I had anticipated he would be.

'Have you got your own copies of the magazines you mentioned?' he asked.

'One of them,' I answered, 'but the others I haven't been published in, and in common with most poets I write poetry but hardly ever read the stuff! I suppose I ought to be ashamed to admit it but I never buy the journals, no idea who does to be honest. It's a miracle the whole enterprise keeps going. So the only copies of magazines I have are those I've been sent as contributor copies, ones I've been published in. I do read those.' I smiled. 'Even the poems of the other contributors.'

Hugo too smiled. 'Much human activity is difficult to comprehend. The things we do all fulfil some need or other, usually our own of course. It's what makes social anthropology so absorbing. I don't suppose you could suggest someone who might have a collection of magazines?'

'You could try the Poetry Library,' I suggested. 'It's on the South Bank.'

'I'll do that,' he said to my surprise. 'If it gives me any ideas I'll pop in and see you tomorrow. You'll be at work?'

'Of course,' I answered somewhat primly. 'Some of us have to apply ourselves day after day to get results instead of flitting about the world occasionally saying 'Oh, that's interesting, I'll write a paper about it'.'

He grinned.

'That sounds to me like an example of the survival of the envious attitude of the first farmers towards the remaining hunter-gatherers. It'd make an interesting study!'

However Hugo didn't appear the next day; instead he telephoned me from King's Cross to say he was returning north. The Poetry Library had been a bust — it happened to be closed for unspecified repairs when he got there. He wasn't sure when he'd next be in London and suggested I go and look instead once it was open again. I demurred.

'I'm inundated with work at the moment and besides I don't know what it is you are looking for.'

'I don't really know myself,' he confessed.

'There are other poetry libraries,' I suddenly remembered, 'much nearer you. The Northern Poetry library is in Morpeth. I don't suppose it is so comprehensive — we both know everything in the North East gets short shrift when it comes to funding — but there's also the Scottish Poetry Library in Edinburgh which I should think is more fortunate in that regard. The Morpeth one is in the public library, at the end of the high street.'

'Oh yes I know Morpeth Library. I suspect it'll be sufficient for my enquiries. Thanks.'

He rang again several days later.

'I can't say I've found any leads browsing through the magazines in the library. Mind you it's a fascinating collection. I'd no idea that sort of stuff existed. It's a treasure trove of raw data for an anthropological study, especially the editors' guidelines for submissions. I did notice that most contributors stuck to definite territories in terms of subject matter and places of publication. I didn't notice you in any of these by the way.' I could sense him smiling mockingly at the other end of the line!

'Does that mean I'm not on your suspect list then?' I asked sarcastically.

'On the contrary, I suspect our quarry, if indeed there is one, will eventually be found among those who weren't in the magazines whose editors were targeted.'

This remark stirred something in my mind but I couldn't quite grasp it at the time.

'So I think we are stuck for the moment,' went on Hugo. 'I will of course let you know if I get any ideas and I assume you'll do the same — let me know if you do that is,' he finished rather pedantically.

I didn't have much hope of inspiration but in fact it wasn't long afterwards that I found myself ringing Hugo although not with an idea.

'There's been another one,' I blurted out without preamble. 'The editor of a magazine I had a submission in to. As it happens it's a slightly unusual one in that it has — had — joint editors and the surviving editor has written to all of us awaiting decisions to let us know there will be a delay. Indeed he says that he may not be able to keep the magazine — *Vista Verse* — going and if any of us want our work returned anyway, to let him know.'

'Where is the editorial address?'

'Durforth-in-Elmet, not far from Leeds.'

'Do you think the surviving editor would be willing for us to visit him?'

'I don't see why he shouldn't. I'll give

you his phone number. Let me know if you do arrange a meeting; I can't guarantee I'll be able to come too; it'll depend when it is.'

When Hugo rang again it was to tell me he'd spoken to the remaining editor of *Vista Verse*, Frank Pearson, and agreed a date and time to visit. Fortunately I was able to free up the day; I said I'd get a train to Leeds and Hugo offered to pick me up at City Station. On the day these arrangements worked smoothly and we were ringing the bell of Pearson's semi-detached bungalow about 11.30 on a fine and bright, though cool morning. The bungalow was one of perhaps a dozen identical buildings with open plan front gardens in a small development, the sort of uninspired housing you can see on the outskirts of uncounted dormitory villages all over the kingdom. Pearson greeted us and ushered us into a smallish living room at the rear of the bungalow from which large patio doors afforded a view of a small but secluded garden. He seemed very subdued and from things he said I realised that the two editors had enjoyed a more intimate partnership than just their editorial one. He offered us coffee which we accepted gratefully and when we were all supplied he asked us what it was we wanted to know. I was happy to leave the explanation to Hugo.

'I don't know if you've noticed but there seems to have been an unusually large number of deaths of small press editors recently.'

Pearson looked aghast.

'What on earth are you talking about?' he asked.

'We are just puzzled, that's all,' replied Hugo. 'I'm a social anthropologist and I study patterns of behaviour or events among human groupings. However it certainly isn't my intention to intrude.' (Clearly Hugo too had sensed the emotional depth of Pearson's grief, as his approach was uncharacteristically solicitous). 'If our interest at this time is too soon or indeed entirely distasteful we won't persist.'

'It's all right,' answered Pearson, 'in fact it is a bit of a relief to talk to someone about Alan's passing.' He looked at me. 'I remember your poems about your loss of your wife. Did you find that following the event people were quick to offer sympathy but then after that initial supportive clustering round were almost as quick to avoid further attention? As though in suffering bereavement you had become a stranger? A different and unknown person?'

I nodded.

'I don't know what causes it,' he went on. 'Embarassment, fear, a feeling that you ought to need solitude to grieve? Whatever the reason — and it is true that some solitude is welcome — the assurance that life continues if not as normal, at least as practical, would be helpful. So I am glad of an opportunity to talk and probably I'm finding it easier with strangers than I would with close acquaintances of both Alan and I. Sorry, I'm going on a bit.'

'Tell us if you will,' said Hugo, 'how the two of you arranged the joint editorship.'

'We both read all submissions and decided separately if we were prepared to accept each one. Then we compared our notes and if we were both for acceptance

the poem went in a provisional acceptance pile; if we were both against then
into a definitely reject pile; and if we were
divided we put it in a possibly reconsider
pile. Those definitely rejected we returned
to their authors straightaway; Alan usually
did that using a standard letter, sometimes with what we hoped were helpful
comments added. If we had accumulated
enough with two votes to fill an issue,
then we also returned those in the divided
pile. Finally we reread and discussed the
two vote ones and agreed which we
should actually use, and then returned
the remainder. We never keep submissions
from one period to the next. It was my
task to decide on the order and layout of
each issue.'

'What stage in the process for the next
issue were you at?' asked Hugo.

'We'd done the initial read and sort and
Alan was sending out the definite
rejections. He still had some to do. If you
come into the study I'll show you.'

We followed him into an adjoining
room. There was a somewhat battered
desk, a comfortable looking desk chair

and another chair to one side. On the desk was a BBC microcomputer with what in retrospect seems a hopelessly boxy monitor, a primitive-looking dot matrix printer and a rotating dial telephone. The only item of equipment which has scarcely changed in appearance since then was a tall grey metal filing cabinet. On the wall opposite the desk was a shelf on which silver cups and other trophies were arrayed. The room looked comfortable and no doubt felt cosy for one person but with the three of us in there it was claustrophobic.

On the desk were three piles of envelopes. They had obviously been slit open but the contents must have been replaced in each.

'We use the submission envelopes to keep things together and ensure we don't get anything muddled,' Pearson confirmed. 'That small pile is the one Alan had nearly finished. I must get the few remaining done but I wrote to all the others first about the delay.'

'Yes,' I said. 'Thank you. That was considerate of you, especially so in such trying circumstances.'

'Do you still have a list of all the rejected submissions?' asked Hugo.

'Yes of course.' Pearson pulled a substantial red backed A4 notebook out of a cubbyhole and handed it to Hugo, who turned to the latest entries. While he perused them Pearson and I engaged in small talk.

'Yours?' I asked, indicating the trophies.

'My father's' he answered. 'He was a school games master and kept very fit himself. Most of these are for amateur athletics events, a few for shooting. I think he found my own lack of sporting prowess a bit disappointing and I was an only child. He did manage to make a reasonable shot out of me although my eyesight meant I could only have competed at short range and really I never felt much interest.'

Hugo interrupted us. He indicated the page of most recent submissions.

'Is there anything unusual about any of these?'

Pearson frowned. 'I don't think so. Especially not that one.' He pointed to a name with the faintest of smiles on his face. 'He regularly submits poems and we invariably reject them.'

Hugo gave him a quizzical look.

'I wouldn't normally say this, but I count on you not to repeat it. His work is terrible — not just badly written cliche-riddled versification, but boring in subject matter as well. It has absolutely nothing to recommend it unless you count the fact that there's never any difficulty about deciding what to do with it. That's not just our opinion; other editors I've met at conferences have commented on it — not all of them are as reticent about would-be contributors as I prefer to be and some of them are devastatingly scathing about his attempts at writing poetry. Yet he keeps submitting, has been doing so for years. I suppose he should be given credit for perseverance. Alan nick-named him the poem-monger. I was even less charitable and called him the verse-monger.' He frowned again.

'Come to think of it there was something odd about him this time. Although we are resigned to the fact that as soon as we send him a rejection he'll send us another submission, this time he actually sent another in before we'd returned the first. What's more, he uses unusual envelopes.' He fished in the waste paper basket under the desk and pulled out an envelope made of a heavy paper that looked hand-made.

'He uses hand-made envelopes fashioned from hand-made paper. Must cost a fortune unless he makes them himself which seems unlikely. Yes I remember now, the first one came in this envelope and the enclosed stamped addressed return envelope was just the same as usual, but the second one although it had a handmade return envelope as usual, arrived in an ordinary cheap envelope. We joked about it, said his standards must be slipping, unkindly comparing the superior character of his envelopes with the terrible quality of his verse.'

'Do you still have the sub-standard envelope? asked Hugo.

'It'll be in there somewhere,' answered Pearson pointing to the basket.

Hugo rummaged through.

'No,' he said finally. 'I couldn't see another envelope with a matching post mark. Of course some of them are very difficult to make out at all, and there are several with other London postmarks from different districts. He might easily have posted it while he was on the move.'

'I can't see it has any significance,' said Pearson. 'He may just have forgotten he'd already sent us something and might quite easily have made up a batch of return envelopes and then run out of his special envelopes when he was getting this submission ready.'

'Hm, possible I suppose.'

'Anyway,' said Pearson, 'you surely aren't suggesting there's something suspicious about Alan's death? What could there be?'

'Don't know,' acknowledged Hugo. 'No reason to think so, it's just that he isn't the only one, that's all when it all comes down to it. Well we mustn't trespass on your good nature any further. You have been very helpful. May I just keep the hand-made envelope? It really is quite a fine one, even used.'

We said our farewells. I lingered a

moment to commiserate once more with Pearson.

'I found after my wife died that it helped the days go by if I kept busy,' I said. 'Not that I had much choice about going to work, but in my free time I found that writing reduced the time I spent brooding. You might find keeping the journal going would do the same for you, and it would be a fitting memorial for Alan if it continues. More appropriate than an inert stone perhaps.'

'Thank you, there's probably sense in what you say. I'll think about it.'

Hugo rather undermined my efforts to offer comforting advice.

'Oh, just one more question. I'm sorry to ask it but was there an autopsy?'

'Yes. It was heart failure.'

'No inquest?'

'No, why should there have been? It's true Alan wasn't old but I understand it does occur even in people younger than us and we didn't keep as fit as perhaps we should have done. My doctor's always on at me to lose weight.'

As we drove back towards the city,

Hugo asked in a thoughtful tone:

'Would it be feasible to lace gum with a poison and coat the flap of an envelope with it?

'Of course,' I answered. 'Cyanide is an obvious choice since the sodium and potassium salts are water soluble making application easy and they are not all that hard to come by nefariously. The trouble is cyanide poisoning exhibits fairly obvious symptoms and is quite quick. It couldn't have been used in this case but I am sure there must be alternatives; I'm not really up in poisons, just any that I might come in contact with in my work. But I'm certain it is a method I've come across being used, if not in real life then in fiction. Can't remember where I read of it though. Are you seriously considering the possibility?'

'We need to visit Norbert Delander, the man who uses hand-made envelopes,' Hugo replied obliquely. I took that to mean he was, and I had to acknowledge that it would explain a lot but it seemed so bizarre in the context of the small press world.

'We should have asked Pearson for his address,' was all I said.

'No need. There was a list of addresses in the back of that register. I memorised Delander's. He lives in London. I was very impressed with how organised those two were. I suppose it's necessary if you run that kind of magazine.'

It was not until the afternoon of the following day that Hugo and I were able to seek out Delander.

No. 25 Terebinth Avenue in Stratford was a substantial mid-terrace house now sub-divided into flats. We climbed the steps to the front door which was ajar. Delander's name was on a slip of card against the bell push for the top flat. Hugo had his finger poised over the bell push when there was a noise like a pistol shot. We looked at each other for a moment and then Hugo pushed at the door which swung inward. He stepped over the threshold.

'You can't Hugo,' I warned, 'I'm sure it's some sort of offence to enter without invitation.'

'The door's open,' he rejoined. 'That's

tantamount to an invitation.' He began to mount the stairs, though I noted he was careful not to touch anything. Reluctantly I followed his example. When we reached the top landing the door of the only flat on that floor was also ajar. Gingerly Hugo toed it further open. He stepped noiselessly through and I felt compelled to follow. There were several doors along the short hall but they were all closed except for the far one immediately opposite the front door. Through this came the sound of sobbing. We approached and looked inside.

It was a small room with a large desk its dominant piece of furniture. Behind it and facing the door was a swivel chair on which sat a man with a beard and wild hair and a look of surprise on his face, presumably Norbert Delander. Three of the walls were lined with shelves reaching to the ceiling and on which were piled books, files and heaps of papers. The word that came irresistibly to mind was den — the place where this character sat and penned his poetry and plotted his revenge on those who rejected it. At an angle to the front of the desk was an upright chair on which sat the source of the weeping. Delander pointed at the figure.

'He shot at me,' he exclaimed in an outraged voice.

At this the other man straightened up, raising his head from where it had been resting on arms crossed on his knees and disclosing that he was Frank Pearson. It also revealed that he was holding a small pistol.

Neither Hugo nor I are medical men, but I couldn't see any sign of injury; no obvious wound or blood.

'Are you hurt?' asked Hugo.

'No, no I don't think so. He just burst in like a madman,' went on Delander. 'Accused me of killing his partner by letter!'

'Your s.a.e was poisoned! I know it was; it's the only explanation — some sort of delayed action poison mixed in the gum on the flap. Here are more of his envelopes — all hand-made. Look!' He pointed dramatically at a pile of them.

'That's ridiculous,' sneered Delander. 'I told him so — told him I didn't do it

76

— why would I? But he pointed the gun at me and fired it!'

Pearson dropped the gun on the floor disgustedly — to my relief.

'It's not loaded,' he said, 'at least, only with blanks: it's a starting pistol. It was my father's.' He aimed a shaking finger at Delander. 'He said Alan's death was a genuine case of poetic justice. And he laughed! Nothing could be more perverse. Alan was such a kind person. He always tried hard to find encouraging words to say even when he knew we had to reject something. His murder was a poetic *injustice*. Anyway what does poetry matter compared with Alan? All the poetry in the world is worth less than he was.' He subsided into a brooding silence. Hugo turned to Delander.

'Did you keep the rejection letter?' he asked.

'The letter, yes, it'll be filed.' He gestured vaguely at a couple of grey filing cabinets behind the door against the only wall not fitted with shelves. 'But not the envelope, if you were thinking of checking it for clues!'

'Pity,' remarked Hugo.

'You're welcome to an unused one.' Delander pointed to a pile of them on the desk.

'Thanks.' Hugo took a couple though he must have realised as I did that they were unlikely to show anything untoward. But I had begun to get the glimmerings of an idea, not a solution but perhaps a way towards one.

'Do you make multiple submissions?' I asked Delander. This is a practice which is a constant source of controversy at all levels of the publishing industry not just the cottage level! (For those not conversant with the practicalities of being an author, it means submitting a given piece of work to more than one publisher at a time instead of waiting for a rejection from one before trying another editor). Most editors deplore it and I think most writers respect the proscription either out of courtesy or from a desire not to antagonise editors!

'Of course,' answered Delander, as if only a fool would waste time by adhering to generally accepted norms. I was not overly surprised; it seemed consistent with his other attitudes.

'I assume you keep a record of submissions,' said Hugo.

'Naturally.' Delander was patently impatient with these questions about his working practices but he reached out to a shelf and pulled down one of a set of well-worn thick exercise books. He opened it on the desk in front of him and turned it round so we could read it. The columns gave the date, target magazine, list of poems sent to them on that date, usually half a dozen, and result. Even from a cursory inspection it was obvious he went in for wholesale multiple submissions. I looked through for his last submission to *Vista Verse* but had to go a long way back to find it. It wasn't only that Norbert Delander was so industrious in his submission programme, though he certainly was, but it really had been a long time ago and, puzzlingly, the poems he'd sent didn't match the poems rejected according to entries Hugo had copied from the *Vista Verse* register. I pointed this out to Delander. For the first time he looked unsure of himself.

'Ah, yes, I couldn't understand that myself. The last rejection letter I received from VV was for poems I didn't have a note of having sent. It seems I slipped up for once. I do sometimes get muddled in my head about which poems I've sent where, hence the register, and that's always been one hundred per cent accurate, until just recently.' He turned to the back pages of the register and pointed.

'See, I made a note here of the submission which wasn't recorded when sent.' I looked at it and it did indeed coincide with the poems most recently recorded in the *Vista Verse* ledger. It wasn't the only such entry though. There were several others and with some satisfaction, even excitement, I saw that most of them were from editors recently deceased. I indicated the entries to Delander.

'These are other submissions you hadn't recorded on sending?' I asked, to be absolutely sure my surmise was correct. He nodded unhappily.

'Yes; I don't know why I've made so many mistakes like that lately. It's a bit worrying.'

Perhaps the idea that was trying to come together in my mind was wrong, perhaps it really was Delander, perhaps he was also a victim but of some sort of mental illness precipitated by frustration at constant rejection, and which had blanked out submissions sent with poisoned s.a.e's? But I didn't believe that. Hugo was studying the inserted entries.

'You've put a lower case c with a point after it in front of these entries,' he said to Delander and pointed to a 'c.', 'presumably for circa?'

'Yes, I didn't know exactly when I must have sent them but I could estimate from the turnaround intervals I usually experienced with particular editors.'

Hugo began perusing entries in an earlier part of the register. After a while he stopped and showed Delander an entry.

'There's nothing in the 'result' column here.'

'No that was a bit odd. Walpurg normally sends rejections of my work with almost indecent dispatch but in that case I obviously still haven't received one. At first I took that as a sign that he was giving it favourable consideration but as more and more time has gone by I've assumed something has gone wrong.'

'Do you chase them up?' I asked.

'After six months I send an enquiry as to whether the submission was received. That one is nearly due for chasing.'

Hugo entered the details in his notebook and then continued working backwards through the register. After a while he again asked about an entry.

'This one says 'Lost in the post' in the results column.' Delander nodded.

'I remember that one. I wrote to Walpurg after waiting six months for a reply and had a letter back to say he hadn't received my submission. It had happened with him before and I was beginning to suspect that he just wasn't properly organised and that he'd received my poems and simply lost them.' I was beginning to think I might have been on the right track earlier after all, and the idea was beginning to take a more definite shape in my mind. Hugo went on searching for a while but made no further notes. At length he sat back.

'Thank you,' he said to Delander. 'That register is very helpful. It looks to me very much as though you've been set up.'

'Why?' he asked in astonishment.

'Probably just because he could use you for his purpose, whatever that is.'

'I take it you're talking about Walpurg?'

'Yes, but I've no reason to think he has any special interest in you, it may be that you just provided the weapon he needed.'

'Weapon?'

'Your submissions strategy.'

Delander shook his head.

'I don't understand what you're talking about. Why don't you just go away and take that maniac with you.' He stabbed a finger towards Pearson.

Hugo rose.

'There are still things I'm not clear about myself,' he admitted. 'We need to investigate further but I promise we'll let you know what we find out. In the meantime make sure you keep that register safe; it may be needed as evidence.'

'You can't have it,' snapped Delander, 'I need it for my work. Just leave and close the door as you go so I can get on with my writing.'

Hugo and I said brief goodbyes; Pearson mumbled an apology of sorts as he picked his gun off the floor.

As we stood in the street outside the house I gestured at Delander's window.

'Not an attractive person,' I remarked.

'Perhaps he considers discourtesy a perquisite or even a prerequisite of genius,' Hugo smiled. He turned to Pearson. 'We'll accompany you to Kings Cross,' he said.

'You don't need to make sure I'm leaving London,' rejoined Pearson huffily. 'I behaved stupidly. I realise that; I won't repeat my mistake.'

'No, no,' Hugo reassured him, 'that isn't it at all. I need to return to Newcastle myself.' So we all three got the underground to the main line station. I tagged along as Hugo's initial remark had clearly included me and I assumed he planned to discuss his deductions with me, although in fact I could see the direction he was following myself.

'You will let me know the result of your enquiries won't you,' said Pearson. 'I want to know who and why, but I'll be content with your assurance that justice will be done. I won't try to dispense it myself.'

'I promise,' replied Hugo.

Sitting in the station buffet after the Leeds train had departed, I tackled Hugo.

'We can't risk any more fiascos like that,' I said firmly. 'We must tell the police what we know and what we suspect.' Hugo considered for a moment. He seemed unduly solemn.

'I fear you are right for once,' he conceded, 'but it is all rather nebulous. I fancy we'd get short shrift at the local cop shop. I think the best thing would be to seek Sebastian's advice.'

'I'll come with you,' I said. I could see the force of Hugo's argument and his suggested approach sounded politic — asking for advice rather than demanding action, but I wanted to hear for myself that Sebastian heard it all, and no more; Hugo has been known to select and to embellish data! He's a consummate impromptu storyteller unlike me. Besides I was the equivalent of the 'local expert', having experience of the small press world which neither Hugo nor Sebastian did. And of course I wanted to find out what happened at first hand!

Hugo glanced at his watch.

'I really need to get back tonight,' he said, 'I wonder if we could get to see him now.' Abruptly he rose and went out onto the concourse. With a sigh I followed him; I'd hoped to get back to College and have at least some work done to show for the day.

'He didn't sound very pleased to hear from me,' said Hugo when at last he turned from the public telephone. The thought seemed to cheer him up rather than the reverse. 'We'd better get a taxi. Like us he's pressed for time as usual.'

Some time later we sat in Sebastian Sinclair's office at Scotland Yard and I listened while Hugo related events in his most persuasive manner, concluding with a concise summary of his exposition:

'Walpurg contrived to acquire Delander's s.a.e.s by using replacement envelopes to return Delander's submissions or simply failing to return them at all. The Delander poems he didn't return he sent on to his victims accompanied by a Delander s.a.e, the flap of which he first coated with gum admixed with poison.'

When he'd finished Sebastian turned to me.

'What do you think?' he asked me.

'Knowing what I do of the small press world, I feel Hugo's deductions are sound.'

Sebastian made one of those exclamations of exasperation which are difficult to represent on paper.

'Sound deductions don't always equate to the truth unfortunately. Where's the motive? Supposing I concede that the modus operandi is feasible, what is the point of the killings? Even if the perpetrator is a maniac, he must have some sort of deranged reason for what he's doing.'

'I don't know,' I admitted, 'but it can't be financial. There's no money in the small presses. It'd have to be personal I should think.'

'But you can't be more specific than that?' he asked caustically.

'No.' I reflected. 'There is someone I could ask who might have an idea though.'

'And who is this oracle?'

'He's called Sean Thurrock. Could I use your phone?'

Sebastian pushed it across the desk towards me and I dialled. It seemed to ring for a long time.

'He might not answer even if he's there,' I said to the others. 'He doesn't like telephones.'

Sinclair rolled his eyes theatrically heaven-ward, but at that moment Sean picked up.

'Hello,' I said, 'it's Alex — Alexander Dunkley. Sorry to ring you but it's urgent.' I heard his musical Welsh accent; it sounded a long way away. I explained the problem as briefly as I could, helped by the fact that we'd discussed the beginnings of the whole affair in letters. His answers were to the point but hardly conclusive.

'Sean says there's long been a bitter dispute between Walpurg on the one side and a number of other small presses, including all the victims and a number of others as well, on the other. It's a literary argument at bottom, but over the years it's taken on a seriously personal tone. In essence Walpurg accused the others of debasing poetry by publishing old-fashioned hack verse, whereas he espouses the philosophy that true poetry does not need rhyme or rhythm, scansion or even sense, not only does not need them but abjures them. Sean was at a conference of independent presses where the argument boiled over, degenerating into ill-natured personalities and abuse. The quarrel has continued to simmer in the pages of some magazines ever since. The most vocal opponents of Walpurg's views included all those who have died recently and seemingly rather before their time. In fact, he says, of the most prominent only Charlie Hart editor of *Scenes Seen* remains.' I paused, then resumed: 'I'm feeling rather glad now that I never attended any of these jamborees; they sound even less attractive than chemical congresses.'

Sinclair looked at the notes he'd made. 'That does all dove-tail with your speculations,' he conceded. 'If they have any substance, this Charlie Hart would appear to be at risk too. I think from that point of view as well as to get as much evidence as possible connecting the crimes with Walpurg, it would be sensible to go and see him without delay. It's not all that convenient but crime rarely is. Do you know where he lives?'

'I'll have to look it up. I know I have the address because I have occasionally sent him stuff, but I don't actually remember it. I think it's in Brighton.'

'You still living in the Chilterns?'

I nodded.

'Right. I don't want to make a big fuss about this in case it's a mare's nest, so I'll sign out an unmarked car and I'll drive it myself. We'll go to your place and get this address, and hope it's not too far afield. Wherever it is though, we'd better go straight away just in case. Do you think you might have a telephone number as well?'

I shook my head. 'The small presses are not all that keen on telephoning.'

'So I gathered,' said Sinclair a trifle grimly.

'I need to get back north,' said Hugo.

'Then you'd better hope this doesn't take long,' responded Sinclair. 'I shall need both of you along if this enquiry is to carry any conviction.' We all ignored the unintended pun at the time.

We headed out of London on the M40 to High Wycombe whence we turned north into the hills where I had my cottage. Once there I quickly found the address and it was indeed in Brighton which wasn't too much of a journey. We retraced our route to Wycombe and back to the M25 to the M23, the road to the south coast. We were entering Brighton not much more than an hour later.

Sebastian broke what had been a long silence.

'I started out here as a detective constable after my first years in uniform. I hope I can remember my way around.'

In fact he made unerringly for the address, which was not far from the front, in a pleasant square with a railed garden in its centre. He quickly located a parking place in an adjacent street and we walked back to the square. The houses round it were imposing town houses, most now divided into flats from basement to attic. We found the number we needed.

'Leave the talking to me unless I cue you in,' requested Sinclair and he pressed the button next to a name card on which was typed C. Hart.

A speaker phone spluttered into life and a woman's voice answered.

'Who is it?'

'I'm Inspector Sinclair of the Metropolitan Police, and I have two colleagues with me. I'm looking for Charlie Hart. I'm hoping he can help us with some enquiries.' There was a short pause before the voice came again.

'Would you hold your identification in front of the camera please.'

There was a small lens above the bell pushes and Sebastian held his warrant card close to it.

'Okay,' said the voice, and there was the sound of the door lock releasing. We trooped inside and climbed the stairs to the third floor. Sinclair pressed the bell of the flat we needed. It was opened on a chain and an eye looked through the gap. It was pushed to again, there was the sound of the chain being removed and then the door opened wide.

'Come in please. I'm Charlie Hart — the Charlie is short for Charlotte.'

I was surprised although I shouldn't have been. I had no real reason to think she was a man and not a woman except that Charlie is more often the diminutive of Charles than Charlotte. I'd sent stuff to the magazine but, like most of the editors I attempted to interest in my work, I'd never met her. She was a woman in perhaps her early thirties. I'm hopeless at gauging ages — I see people as a whole not as an assembly of attributes and my overall impression of her was as an attractive simply dressed youngish woman.

'We are sorry to disturb you,' began Sebastian, 'we won't waste more of your time than we can help but this may be a serious matter.' He indicated Hugo and me.

'This is Dr Hugo Lacklan and Dr Alexander Dunkley.' Charlie Hart regarded me with interest.

'The poet?' she asked. That's the sort of remark which still gives me a warm glow of satisfaction, as though confirmation that someone else considers what I write is proper poetry — like seeing my poems in print. I suppose this is actually a clear indication that I still don't feel confident in the worth of my writing! But realising that doesn't dispel the pleasure I feel.

Sinclair was clearly anxious to press on.

'Does a Norbert Delander send you poetry to consider?'

Charlie Hart sighed.

'Yes,' she answered shortly.

'Do you have any currently, or any un-opened mail which might be from him?'

She reflected.

'None that I haven't already rejected unless there are some in the pile from the last few days — I've been away.'

'May we have a look please?'

'Of course.'

She led us through to a big room at the back of the building. Large windows filled the space with sky. It was comfortably furnished but not crowded with possessions. She let down the flap of a bureau and from a compartment extracted a bundle of mail fastened with an elastic band.

'I removed the obvious bills and junk mail,' she remarked. She offered the bundle to Sinclair who took from his pocket a pair of surgical gloves and donned them expertly before accepting it. Charlie Hart's eyes widened.

'My god!' she exclaimed. 'You really do think this is something serious.'

'It may be, or it may not. If there's any question about it, it's best to follow standard procedures.' He delicately sorted through the unopened envelopes, selected three, and placing the rest on the flap of the bureau, fanned the three and showed them to Charlie Hart.

'All right if I open these?' She nodded.

He took a paper knife from the bureau and neatly slit open the envelopes and peered inside each, finally selecting one and placing the others on the flap. He inserted the two longest fingers of one hand into the envelope with the deftness of a pickpocket and extracted several sheets of typed poems and a hand-made envelope.

'That's from Norbert Delander,' exclaimed Charlie. 'I recognise the s.a.e, but it hasn't come in a similar one like it usually does.'

'Which means,' said Sinclair, 'that if my colleagues' theory is correct you may have had a narrow escape. They think these submissions purporting to come from Delander but in different envelopes to those he usually uses, are in fact from Daniel Walpurg.'

Expressions of understanding followed by puzzlement crossed Charlie's face.

'Is this something to do with recent deaths of editors of magazines?'

'Why would you think that?' asked Sinclair.

'I'm not sure but you mentioning someone who had quarrelled with quite a few of them and you coming here to see me with whom he also quarrelled and your circumspect handling of my mail as if it might be dangerous or at least evidence, all seem to suggest something like that. People have been speculating about the seeming epidemic of deaths. I don't pretend to follow what is in your mind but it seems certain that all these things are connected in some way.'

'I need to take this letter and contents

away,' said Sinclair. 'I'll give you a receipt for it and if you receive any more of a like kind please let me know straight away and I'll arrange to have them collected by the local police and passed on to me.' He handed her his card. Shortly afterwards, we left.

When we got back to London Sebastian said he would take the matter from there and warned us in particular to stay away from any of the people who seemed to be involved and not to communicate with any of them. So what happened next wasn't in any way the fault of Hugo or myself. I feel sure Sinclair moved with what speed he could but there were other police forces to be involved with all the usual ramifications of protocol and then the raid on Walpurg's house to be organised and set in train and in the event it came too late as Sebastian eventually related to me in a somewhat strained interview.

Whatever Sebastian may or may not have suspected, I didn't tell Pearson anything about what we had discovered or suspected and nor did Hugo I'm sure.

He'd have admitted it if he had. No, Pearson must have worked it out for himself from what he heard Hugo and I saying at Delander's place. The starting pistol wasn't the only gun of his father's he'd inherited; there was also a competition pistol. Sinclair only gave me a brief outline of what ensued. Pearson had gone to Walpurg's (seen by neighbours and subsequently identified by them against police photographs). He'd knocked and been invited in. Shortly afterwards, something that could have been a shot was heard, and almost immediately after that Pearson left the house and drove off. When the local police arrived they found Walpurg dead, shot through the heart.

A small boy loitering in the street had been playing at cops and robbers and noting everything going on in the street before bedtime! The registration number of the car Pearson had driven away in was something he'd recorded in his notebook and suffused with importance he'd told the policeman standing guard outside Walpurg's house while his senior colleagues were inside. The Vehicle Licensing

Centre had revealed its ownership. Once again though, events moved too fast. By the time police arrived at Pearson's bungalow they had to break in. They found him in the study chair, dead, his head on his arms on the desk. The bottle of pills he'd used to release him from his misery was there too, and alongside it a single sheet of paper on which he had written an unrhymed quatrain:

> Poetry was our life,
> poetry was his death.
> We lived for each other;
> I die alone.

Sebastian said there would of course be investigations of all the deaths which were now deemed suspicious and inquests probably on most of them as well as on Walpurg and Pearson. He was confident that the verdicts would be unlawful killing if not simply murder and that they would probably opt to name Walpurg and Pearson respectively as the perpetrators, which would effectively close the cases since both of them were dead.

I now come to the really unsatisfactory aspect of this account and the reason I have waited so long before seeking its publication — the nature of the poison used. The mode of administering the poison — coating the flap of an envelope with poisoned gum — is far from unknown in both fact and fiction. A popular poison has been cyanide but as I explained to Hugo that couldn't have been used in this instance. Sinclair said that although the poison used might be named at the inquests, the Crown Prosecutor would endeavour to avoid that for fear of making copycat killings too easy, unless it was deemed absolutely necessary to secure a verdict, which seemed unlikely. Sebastian advised me fairly insistently that it would in the circumstances be irresponsible for me to name it. This seemed to me a bit farfetched. Although there had been arguments in the scientific literature about the advisability or not of publishing scientific papers reporting research on gene recombination and modification in relation to the creation of more deadly forms of diseases, such as flu which have potential as biological weapons and might seem attractive to terrorists, such considerations were hardly applicable in this case.

Sinclair fell back on that old debating point that if only one person were to die as the result of my divulging the name I would bear some of the blame and more importantly a person would be dead who might otherwise still be alive. It's an argument to which there are well-rehearsed counter arguments but in the end I decided, perhaps pusillanimously, to accede to his urging even though I myself subsequently found it reasonably easy to work out the most likely reagent, as of course Walpurg must have done. I feel strongly that its omission detracts from the integrity of the account, and that I am behaving unprofessionally by omitting it. It offends my scientific training to withhold an essential fact. Nevertheless I have given in and must ask you to accept that this was the method and that it is in fact viable. That I have decided to publish now, though without identifying the poison, is because in the years that have passed since then, the internet has come into being and almost any fact is discoverable on line with very little in the way of prior knowledge being necessary. So I feel I don't need to delay any longer.

As usual Hugo had the last word, in this case a last question which he addressed to me.

'So which of your two interests would you judge the more dangerous; chemistry or poetry?'

The Enigma of the Speeding Toadstool

Although its inception was so light-hearted, the enigma of the speeding toadstool proved to be as serious as any that Hugo led me into.

We had been walking the wild fells north of Hadrian's Wall and as we headed back to less lonely countryside Hugo was for once driving at a non-alarming pace and I was relaxing as he negotiated the lanes' twists and turns and was enjoying the varied views of the Simonside Hills thus afforded. As we headed into a wooded area a truck shot out of a side road just ahead of us and accelerated away.

'Maniac!' observed Hugo, although it was exactly the sort of manoeuvre he normally perpetrates himself. I was inclined to agree with him although not on account of the driver's shortcomings as a driver but because of the unusual load secured by ropes to the flat bed of the lorry. It appeared to be a toadstool, bright red with white spots, but about eight feet high.

'Follow that toadstool,' I cried facetiously, though I later wished I hadn't.

'What do you know about fly agarics?' asked Hugo.

'Not a lot,' I answered. 'Taxonomic name *amanita muscaria*.'

Hugo glanced at me in surprise. I felt rather smug — I don't often manage to startle him.

'Are you a mycologist as well as a chemist?' he enquired.

Having a deep-seated aversion to any kind of dissembling, something which is a severe handicap if you want to impress people, I admitted that I was not and that I just happened a short while ago to have done some research on natural products derived from the species. The rather odd fact that it concentrates the metal vanadium had been the focus of my interest but perhaps the fascination of this is only comprehensible to those as thoroughly marinated in chemistry as I am so I didn't elaborate. Instead I continued.

'They are a fairly common fungus, typically about three inches high, very poisonous as well as hallucinogenic mainly due to the psychoactive compound muscimol and they don't usually move as fast as the specimen in front.'

Hugo grinned.

'So you think that one is unusual enough for us to take an interest in?'

'Oh no!' I protested. 'You're not going to involve me in some wild toadstool chase.'

Hugo collects the unusual, both professionally — he is a social anthropologist — and as a hobby and has too often embroiled me in time-consuming investigations of odd, even bizarre, occurrences — like the enigma of the benevolent banker, though that's a tale to which I suspect the world is not yet ready to give credit.

'There's bound to be some boring run-of-the-mill explanation of this.' I was keen to get back to London that night, which meant relying on Hugo to deliver me to a main-line station, preferably Newcastle, while there were still trains running that would do that.

'Suggest three possible dull explanations,' demanded Hugo. I thought rapidly.

'It's a theatre prop, or it's destined for a children's playground, or — or it's part of an advertising campaign!' I finished triumphantly.

'Hm! Not bad,' conceded Hugo.

'Your turn,' I said maliciously.

'It's part of a scam, or a plot or a fraud,' he replied promptly.

'Two of those are just synonyms,' I objected. 'Anyway I can't imagine any plot or fraud that would involve the use of a giant toadstool.'

'Nor I,' said Hugo, which surprised me as, even if true, it wasn't his style to admit such a thing.

'So,' he continued, 'it is definitely worth looking into.'

I realised I'd been out-manoeuvred.

Hugo had accelerated to keep the fleeing fungus in view. Of a sudden, the truck's brake lights flared, causing Hugo to stamp on the Range Rover's brakes, and without other signal the driver executed a sharp left turn into an even narrower lane which ran like a tunnel into the thick forest now bordering the road. Hugo cursed, screeched to a halt, backed up and then turned left in its wake onto a single track side-road with passing places, and with grass growing in the middle of the metalling in places.

'That signpost pointed to Scatterdene Woods,' I remarked.

'I noticed. It's a no through road and I can't think of anywhere along it that could possibly interest the transporter of a large toadstool.' Hugo had now dropped back, well away from our quarry and we glimpsed it only intermittently so we were lucky (though that wasn't how I felt at the time) to catch sight of it making another abrupt left turn. Hugo accelerated and then slowed as he approached the spot where the truck had turned. There was no sign of another lane but a few broken branches and a gouge in the soft verge pin-pointed the spot where the vehicle had turned off the highway and into the trees. Hugo hesitated and then drove on for about a hundred yards until he reached a passing place where he pulled as far to the left as he could so that he wasn't blocking the road.

'Come on,' he said, jumping out and closing his door with a careful click. I followed reluctantly. We walked back along the lane to where the truck had entered the wood. Hugo led the way into the gloom of the firs, carefully keeping a bit to one side of the tyre tracks, and leaving no prints in the springy cushion of pine needles. We seemed to be following an old forest way through the trees deeper into an oppressive silence such as only coniferous plantations seem to generate, a dead silence, a secret, permanent silence.

We didn't have far to go before we spied the truck. It was stationary at the nearer edge of a clearing surrounded by deciduous trees and rhododendron bushes. The toadstool had been unloaded and positioned in the middle of the glade where its bright red gleamed in the sun shining through the break in the tree canopy, the big white spots stark against the red in a somehow sinister realisation of an illustration in a child's book of fairy stories.

An overalled figure carried a basket from the lorry towards the toadstool. The contents clinked. He put the basket down on the grass while he opened a door in the stalk of the fungus, picked the basket up again and ducked through the low doorway. After a few minutes, he re-emerged, took the now empty basket back to the vehicle and tossed it in the back. He opened the cab door and retrieved a hessian bag, said a few words to his mate, slammed the door, and stepped back.

The truck reversed out of the glade, presumably back towards the lane. The remaining workman took off his cap, shook out a mass of shoulder-length blonde hair and stripped off his boiler-suit. He rolled it up and as he stuffed that and the cap into the bag, he half-turned and it was clear from the face that he was in fact a woman. Removal of the coverall had revealed she was dressed in a white blouse and slacks. Taking a pair of women's sensible shoes from the bag, she pulled off the boots and replaced them with the shoes, standing easily on one leg to complete the operation. She turned and strode off along a broad grass path leading out the other side of the glade.

Hugo waited a minute or two and then crossed to the toadstool; I followed less certainly. The door wasn't locked. (The very idea was of course ridiculous. My mind seemed to be in some sort of unresolved quantum state, seeing the toadstool both as a growing fungus and as a small building.)

Hugo pulled the door open, ducked, and stepping inside the stalk, straightened up again. I could see his legs turn his body round slowly before he re-emerged.

'Have a look,' he invited.

'Really Hugo,' I remonstrated, 'this isn't one of your investigations, this is sheer nosy-parkering.'

'It's interesting though,' he smiled. With a sigh I did as he said, anxious just to get back on the road and reach Newcastle.

Inside the cap of the toadstool it was fitted out as a miniature room with a table, chairs, cupboards, shelves and even a child sized bed with its head against the curving wall. Above me a window in the dome let in light. On the shelves were books, crockery, boxes, packets and a line of labelled bottles. It had all the appearance of a

110

singularly well equipped play house. I withdrew, noting as I did, the ladder affixed to the inside of the stalk. I confronted Hugo.

'I was right. It's a children's playhouse, an impressive one I'll grant you, but that is all it is. Now can we go back to the real world? I need to catch a train.'

Almost as though he hadn't heard what I'd said, Hugo asked:

'Have you got a specimen tube or small bottle with you?'

'No I haven't,' I replied with some asperity, 'I'm not a mad scientist out of a trashy story; my pockets are not stuffed with chemicals and apparatus; no real scientist has pockets full of test tubes — well perhaps one or two if he's in his lab coat, but in case you hadn't noticed I'm not in uniform today! Anyway what do you want it for?'

As too often in the past, my curiosity was my undoing. The smile on Hugo's face broadened — he knew he had me suckered.

'You saw the bottles? Did you sniff their contents?'

'Really!' I protested weakly.

'The one labelled *Dreams of Faerie* especially? No? It was — suggestive. You wait here and keep watch; I've got a few empty specimen vials in the car I'm sure. I'll only be a few minutes.'

He was off, ignoring my protest.

The silence enveloped me as he disappeared between the trees in the direction of the Range Rover. I looked round. Keep watch indeed! There was nothing to see except for the serried ranks of trees and the surreal form of the gigantic toadstool.

Feeling uneasily exposed standing there in the glade I, quite illogically, set off towards the path leading out of it, the one taken by the woman. It curved away through what quickly transformed into a shrubbery, leaving the tall spindly pines behind. I welcomed the sunshine for its brightness and its warmth. Shortly the path opened out onto a lawn and I hung back, hoping to remain inconspicuous. I stared across the grass at the old house beyond. Somehow it didn't have the appearance of a house where there were children. It was hard to say why but certainly there were no discarded toys lying about, no clutter of any sort, no sounds. It was a gloomy example of Victorian gothic and as silent as the sinister wood. I started as the word sinister slipped into my mind but it seemed entirely appropriate.

I quickly returned to the glade and was glad when Hugo got back. He reinserted himself into the toadstool and in a moment or two backed out again grasping a small tube filled with amber liquid. He flipped up the cap and held it out to me.

'Have a sniff,' he invited. I did so gingerly, for a chemist learns early in his career (if he doesn't want it to be a very short one) not to breathe too enthusiastically of the unknown. However this was in fact quite pleasant. I dipped the tip of my little finger in and equally gingerly tasted it with the tip of my tongue.

'Brandy,' I said in surprise, 'at least that's my impression. Although there is a hint of something else there,' I added reflectively. Hugo nodded.

'It was in the bottle labelled *Dreams of Faerie*; not really what you'd expect in a children's playhouse!'

I had to agree; the toadstool house was looking more and more like an adult fantasy.

'You'll analyse this specimen?' Hugo half queried, half commanded!

'I'm not an analytical chemist.'

'But you have colleagues who are?'

'Yes, yes, all right.' I was now intrigued myself — it was that half-recognised lurking taste.

'Straight away if possible,' he insisted. 'I've a bad feeling about this whole set-up.'

'Very well, if it means I can get the next train back to London!'

We returned to the car, Hugo backed it onto the lane and we set off.

'Isn't this the wrong way? The sign said the lane was a dead end.'

'It's a no through road,' corrected Hugo. 'The sign is right but fails to reveal that it's because it loops back on itself in another half mile or so and eventually rejoins itself before the junction with the main road. I had a look at the map.'

Sure enough the lane soon veered to the left and very soon I sensed we were travelling back in the direction we'd come. Abruptly Hugo slowed the car.

'There it is,' he pointed, 'the front of the house whose back you saw.'

It was set well back from the lane and looked more pretentious from this side as seen through the open gateway but the only sign of life was a red sports car parked on a broad stretch of gravel in front of it. The garden was bounded by a hedge and at one end of this a discreet notice board was instantly recognisable as an estate agents sign. As we passed I noted the agent's name and I presume Hugo did too. After that he accelerated and we were soon hurtling along as he resumed his normal driving style.

The next day was a Monday and as soon as I got to the Chemistry Department I rang Martin Maclean, a colleague in the analytical group and a friend of many years. I explained what I wanted.

'Sure, bring it along,' he replied. 'No use resisting if it's Hugo behind it after all. I've got a student for whom it'll be a nice exercise. I'll phone you with the result.'

When he got back to me he sounded unusually serious and said he'd come along to see me. He arrived in a matter of minutes.

'I don't like this at all,' he said. 'By rights I ought to report it direct to the police. What on earth have you been doing?'

He sat down in the chair on the opposite side of my desk.

'It isn't quite as you suggested. It is indeed a solution in brandy of a psychoactive drug, but that tube contains a lethal concentration of morphinediacetate.'

I pursed my lips.

'Heroin!' I said.

Of course I'd been brooding on the matter and was already prepared to hear something unpalatable and had decided what I would do next. I rang Hugo. Martin settled back in his chair and regarded me thoughtfully. Hugo's departmental secretary Mrs Desai answered. I'd met her during the enigma of *The Indian Ladder Trick*.

'Can I speak to Hugo please, it's very

urgent,' I requested after exchange of the customary greetings.

'I'll see if I can find him.' He came on the line quite quickly. He must have been awaiting the call. I told him the news, including Martin's anxiety about his results.

'Right,' said Hugo, 'I've been doing some phoning around up here and I've formed a theory about what is going on. I do agree that we need to involve the constabulary, but the local force here have a somewhat jaundiced view of me — no don't ask me now, I'll tell you why some other time — but I think the best thing is for me to phone Sebastian. Can you stay within reach of a phone for a while? I may have to ring you back.' (Hugo can't be bothered with mobile phones).

Sebastian Sinclair was a former student of Hugo's and now a senior officer in the Metropolitan Police. I'd first met him at a conference attended by Hugo and I, as well as by Sinclair, and the meeting led to the resolution of the enigma of *The Vanishing Punk*. I told Martin what Hugo had said and explained who

Sinclair was. He seemed placated.

'I'll write up the analysis and let you have it. I rely on you to pass it on to the police.' I promised to do so.

When Hugo rang again he told me Sebastian had been promoted to superintendent and transferred back to East London so that his bailiwick now included my college and he was taking the matter seriously enough to send a car to take me and Martin Maclean into his office. I exclaimed in exasperation — I had work to do! But Martin was relieved when I told him — he would clearly like to get the analysis off his mind and see for himself that a proper report was made! Ten minutes later the porter on the front door of the department rang.

'The police have come for you Dr Dunkley,' he said. Ever since it became generally known that I was a friend of Hugo, I'd been regarded as some sort of eccentric and therefore a fair target for levity. 'They asked for Dr Maclean as well. Shall I ring him?'

Martin and I met in the lobby and accompanied the uniformed constable out to the patrol car. I quite enjoyed the journey to Sinclair's nick, lights and siren affording us comparatively rapid passage through the congested streets of the East End, though I couldn't see that our trip was that urgent.

Sinclair asked me to tell him exactly what had happened and what I'd seen. I gave him the specimen tube and Martin reported his results.

'We'll do our own analysis here,' Sinclair said to Martin, 'not that I doubt your competence but it's a matter of the chain of evidence. I'd also like a copy of your report and a formal statement from both of you. You won't mind making your own way back I hope?'

I wouldn't have said no to another trip in a police car but reflected it might be better not to wish too fervently for that in case the next occasion was less benign! As it was, Martin and I journeyed in the gloom of an almost empty Metropolitan Line train rattling through the stygian tunnels to Stepney Green.

I rang Hugo and brought him up to date.

'Now' I said, 'clue me in on exactly what you've found out up there?'

'Ah, you are speaking crime writer lingo! Right, there's really not much to tell so far. After I left you at the station I made a few enquiries but a Sunday evening is a frustrating time for investigations. Most of them had to wait until today. I did see the estate agent yesterday, the one whose board was outside the house. He didn't know much and all I could learn in my guise of possible purchaser was that the house is lived in by two unmarried sisters and that it belongs to the elder, Miss Ariadne Trevelyan. This morning I spoke to the editor of the local rag, The Advertiser, but he could tell me nothing at all — they clearly have no newsworthiness as far as he knows. Then I thought of the local public library. You know, people underestimate the value of the less advertised sources of information in libraries, the amount of gossip that the librarians themselves accumulate about their customers! They get to meet many of the people in their locality. They may only exchange a few words with them at each encounter, the time it takes to check books in and issue new ones, but they see them again and again, often over a long period, and they notice what sort of books are borrowed. People ask them about books and they tend to remember the more unusual ones.'

'I don't doubt they remember you,' I interjected as he paused to collect his thoughts. He ignored my comment.

'I looked in at libraries in Wooler, Alnwick and Berwick,' he went on, 'and I spoke to one assistant who remembered the Trevelyan sisters well. It was the elder who made most use of the library on a regular basis. She was particularly interested in that area of the occult pertaining to what are often derisively termed 'the little people', most especially fairies, elves, pixies, hobgoblins and the like.'

Things started to fall into place in my mind with that thud of finality exhibited by the operation of old-fashioned railway signal box levers.

'Of course,' said Hugo, 'the study of people's belief in such beings is a significant sub-division of my own subject

121

so tracking down the next clue was perhaps easier for me than it might have been for someone like you for instance, unless like Conan Doyle you'd been inveigled into giving credence to the existence of such creatures yourself. Anyhow I discovered that the elder sister was a regular attendee at the meetings of a local society of like-minded enthusiasts. I located one of them and talked to him.

'I learned that Miss Trevelyan the elder was generous with her financial support for the club and, much more significantly, made no secret of her resolve to sell her house so that she could move into a some-what smaller property closer to Alnwick, and to donate any surplus from the sale to a national organisation dedicated to the study of the faery realm.

'Whilst in the library I'd also asked what the younger sister was interested in and again the answer was most revealing. Her passion was the theatre and from time to time she ordered sets of drama texts from the library for use by a local theatre company. I asked if she knew which it was. She replied that of course she did as that was something that had to be recorded. It was The Cheviot Thespians. I won't bore you with a blow by blow account of my investigation of the theatre group, but there was a member of the company who was at great pains to deny that she was in any way a gossip and so of course was exactly that and from her I learnt that Miss Selena Trevelyan, the younger of the two sisters, had recently become increasingly chummy with the company's props man. And as my informant confided to me, 'he can make anything, he can', I surmise that he will have been responsible for the making of the toadstool and its furnishings. That's how matters stand at the moment but I think it is already evident that some action needs to be taken urgently and I am hoping Sebastian can precipitate it.'

Hardly had Hugo rung off than the phone went once more. This time it was the porter.

'The police have come for you again Dr Dunkley,' he announced with some relish and then, clearly turning towards someone at his end, 'No, wait, you can't just . . . ', but evidently they had. He returned his attention to me.

'Sorry sir, they're on their way up.'

'No need to worry Harry,' I assured him.

A few minutes later there was a brief rap on the door and it opened immediately to reveal Sebastian and a uniformed policeman.

'Sorry to burst in but we're in a hurry. I'd be obliged if you'd come along with us,' he said with just a suggestion of a grin to indicate he was enjoying his self-parody of the plod.

'Where to?' I asked.

'Northumberland.'

'But I . . . '

'You won't need anything,' he assured me, 'but time presses. You should get back tonight.'

So I went. I got my wish of another trip in a police car, though it was rather more than I'd bargained for — three and a half hours of it. That meant we averaged ninety miles an hour and so on the easier stretches of the Great North Road we must have reached considerably more as it was inevitably slower both threading our way out of the East End to start with and in the far north on the still single carriageway stretches of the A1 north of Newcastle. The driver was no doubt very good but frightening was the word that came most readily to mind, and for much of the way as well as the flashing light she had the siren on. Sebastian fell asleep as soon as we were out of London. The driver caught my eye in the mirror. She had nice eyes but I'd have preferred her to keep them on the road even so.

'He conducted a dawn swoop this morning,' she confided quietly, smiling. I reflected that her words could be interpreted in more ways than one if your mind was inclined to scent ambiguities and I felt a mild envy of Sebastian. I wasn't able to sleep, feeling that almost every minute might be my last and that I wouldn't want to miss it, even though everyone says when it's time to go it's best to go in your sleep!

There was a brief stop at a vestigial service area south of Morpeth to rendezvous with officers of the Northumbrian authority and then we were off once more, now following the Northumbrian cars. Sebastian was awake.

'We're going straight to Scatterdene House,' he said. 'All I'd like you to do is observe and let me know if you see anything different from the last time you were there. Don't get in our way or touch anything please. I know that's self-evident to most people of any intelligence but there's always the odd one, like Hugo, who finds it difficult to hang back, so I have to say it nevertheless.'

'Of course,' I replied. Truth to tell I was surprised to be included as I doubted I'd have anything to contribute. I said as much to Sebastian.

'I'd much rather not be here myself,' he replied, 'and my northern colleagues aren't very happy about my presence either.'

'So why are you here?'

'It's entirely due to Hugo of course. He's so persuasive when talking to you and then as soon as he's gone you realise what he's been saying is ridiculously tenuous. So my opposite number up here contacted me for my opinion, Hugo having studiously dropped my name.'

'And you reassured them?'

'Did I heck! I tried, but nothing would content them but I should embroil myself too.'

'I see,' I said, 'so if it turns out to be a mare's nest and the peace of England is riven by the sound of laughing policemen, it'll be you, the big man from London they'll be laughing at.'

He eyed me grimly.

'You have an unpleasant talent for making things sound worse than I'd realised they were.'

It was my turn to sigh.

'It's Hugo,' I returned. 'When my thoughts turn in his direction, which is as seldom as I can contrive, they are liable to turn dark and bitter.'

'There you go again,' he remarked. 'Dark and bitter used to be my favourite real ale taste. Now you've spoiled it.' Unexpectedly he grinned. 'Perhaps that's the real reason I brought you along; as a companion in misery.' He relapsed into silence until we arrived.

We pulled up in the lane either side of the gap where the path led into the forest, completely blocking the road in both directions, presumably deliberately. Everyone piled out except the drivers and we set off along the path. Hugo had been in one of the other cars but now joined me and fell into step beside me.

'Thought you'd like to be in at the death,' he whispered, a choice of phraseology which seemed to me unfortunate to say the least. A detective touched his arm and put an admonitory finger to his lips. Hugo nodded. We came to the clearing. Hugo had obviously been given instructions in advance. He opened the door of the toadstool and stuck his head inside. A moment later he withdrew it.

'The bottle's gone,' he mouthed silently.

Sebastian nodded and set off along the broad ride towards the back of the house. We came to a terrace. It was now growing late and artificial light glowed through French windows at one end of the house. No curtains had been drawn so we could see the interior clearly whereas we were probably hidden from inside by the gloom of the garden. The two women sat in armchairs with a low table between them, in front of a fireplace where a fire was laid but unlit, the evening being warm. In front of the younger of the two was a decanter and a glass of amber liquid. The elder had a similar glass but in place of a decanter was the bottle labelled *Dreams of Faerie*.

Sebastian didn't hesitate. He took two strides to cross the terrace, grasped the handle of the French windows and pulled it sharply down. The door opened without resistance and he stepped inside with us following. The sisters looked up startled. Sebastian bowed in an anachronistic gesture of courtesy — the tableau seemed to require it, like a stage production of *An Inspector Calls*.

'Please don't be alarmed ladies, and do forgive our intrusion. We are pursuing enquiries and the matter is urgent.'

'Who are you?' demanded the elder sister.

Sinclair held out his warrant card for her inspection.

'Superintendent Sinclair,' he replied, adding as though acting out his role, and with some disregard for strict accuracy, 'of Scotland Yard.'

'And the nature of those enquiries?'

Sinclair stepped closer to the table, as he did so pulling on gloves. He leaned forward and picked up the glass of the elder Miss Trevelyan in one hand and the bottle of *Dreams of Faerie* with the other. He sniffed the glass.

'This,' he replied. He half turned.

'Charlton,' he said. A youngish uniformed constable stepped forward, also donning gloves.

'Secure these,' he commanded, 'and don't spill any.'

'Sir,' replied the constable, although his expression expressed confusion as to exactly how he was to comply.

Sebastian readdressed Miss Ariadne: 'I'll give you a receipt of course but, if what we suspect is true, I doubt whether we will be able to return the items.'

'And just what precisely do you suspect,' she asked icily.

'We believe that the bottle and the glass contain brandy laced with a lethal dose of heroin.'

'Preposterous,' she answered but her

eyes were on the younger sister, as were mine. Selena seemed to react hardly at all although I fancied I did detect a slight rigidity of countenance.

'Of course,' went on Ariadne Trevelyan thoughtfully, 'we know so little about elves or fairies.' She faced Sinclair once more.

'I found the bottle in an elf-house in the woods,' she informed him. 'I was surprised by the size of the house, but I have been misled no doubt by popular misconceptions about what ignorant people derisively call 'the little people'. Prof Tolkien had a much more accurate perception of them than most although he chose to pass his research off as fiction. It is quite believable that a concoction that is deadly to mortals would have a very different effect on immortals, as elves and fairies are, or seemingly so to creatures of such miserably short-lived lives as ourselves. If you are right that this magical beverage would have proved inimical to me then you will deserve and indeed receive my thanks for preventing its consumption, although I think you could have achieved that end with less drama and a more economical use of police manpower.'

Sinclair had listened with commendable patience to this peroration and I noticed that one of his officers was recording it in a note book, presumably in shorthand unless he had a magic pen!

'I'm sorry madam,' answered Sinclair politely, 'but it isn't quite as simple as that.'

I gave him full marks for calling her madam rather than 'You barmy old bat', and immediately mentally chastised myself for indulging in so uncharitable a description.

'Forensic examination of the toadstool has shown it not to be genuine but to be a construct of wood, canvas and paint.' I felt sure the wording 'forensic examination' was pure persiflage on Sinclair's part. We'd broken a piece off the magic mushroom and just looking at it could see how it had been fabricated.

'I'm afraid someone has imposed on you,' he went on. 'Not everyone is as respectful of unorthodox beliefs as I am.'

He looked rather pointedly at Selena Trevelyan. Whether it was this or whether she just realised that events called for a readjustment of her plans, she now turned to her sister.

'I'm sorry,' she said, 'I appreciate you didn't want this to be generally known, but I'm sure we can trust to Mr Sinclair's discretion and unless we tell him the truth he may come to some highly prejudicial conclusion.' She turned towards him. 'My sister uses morphine taken in brandy as a sedative, just as the Victorians used opium in brandy — they called it laudanum. It's rather old-fashioned I know and I suppose it may technically be a bit illegal, but there's no harm in it. Coleridge used it you know, wrote some of his poetry under its influence. You may have heard of Kublai Khan,' she added in a condescending tone, underlying which I nevertheless sensed a note of anxiety. She refaced her sister.

'I'd better tell all,' she went on apologetically, 'before this nonsense gets out of hand.' She switched her attention back to Sinclair, very much the amateur

133

actress now, playing to her audience. 'If you look in the wine cellar inspector you'll find a box full of bottles like the one you've appropriated, but empty. This has been going on for quite a while.'

'Selena!' Ariadne Trevelyan sounded outraged.

'Sorry Aria, but this is all getting a bit heavy. We don't want to be accused of wasting police time. Best to be as helpful as possible even though it is all very irritating.'

Sinclair nodded to the sergeant who left the room, beckoning a constable after him. They returned quite quickly carrying a cardboard box, just as Selena had said, filled with bottles like the *Dreams of Faerie* except these had no labels on. Sebastian picked one out with his gloved hand and, removing the stopper, gingerly sniffed it before passing it to me with an expression that implied I should do the same.

'Smells like the mixture in the bottle from the toadstool,' I said. 'Of course it may not be the same strength; can't expect to estimate just by sniffing.' He nodded. Clearly we'd both had the same thought: if it were the same concentration of heroin and she really had drunk the stuff, even in very small amounts, she wouldn't be calmly sitting in her armchair now.

'You see,' said Selena, 'this has been going on for a while and if that latest bottle really is a dangerous strength it must be the fault of the supplier. It is a good job you somehow found out.' It was an audacious attempt to maintain the fiction of her own non-involvement.

Just then another sergeant, one from the Northumbrian constabulary, came in through the French windows and signalled to Sinclair. They conferred outside for a moment. When Sebastian returned there appeared to be the hint of a smile on his face. He regarded the younger sister reflectively.

'That was a clever little reminder of the mythology surrounding the creation of Kublai Khan to which you treated us earlier,' he began. 'If I were to continue the conceit I might cast Sergeant Shiel in the role of the man from Porlock who interrupted Coleridge's recall of his vision causing him to leave the poem forever unfinished. In this case it is your little fantasy he has interrupted and I'd recommend you emulate the poet and forget all about what you were going to say. You see, we've arrested your accomplice. He doesn't have quite your flair for lying.'

I learned later Sinclair had removed the police cars blocking the lane and instead had concealed three men to keep an eye on the toadstool. They'd seen the props man from the Cheviot Thespians theatre group drive up in his truck and prepare to dismantle and cart away the fake fly agaric. He'd admitted that as soon as Selena Trevelyan knew that her sister had found the monstrous fungus and taken away the bottle of *Dreams of Faerie*, she'd phoned him to let him know it was time to remove the prop. They wanted to leave no evidence of the charade they'd played to deceive her sister and so leave only the bottles in the cellar to suggest the tragic accident suffered by Ariadne.

The face of the elder Miss Trevelyan

which had assumed a stony aspect during Selena's mendacious disclosure of Ariadne's alleged laudanum addiction remained unmoved even by these latest revelations.

'I must ask you to accompany me to the station to continue this interview,' Sinclair said to Selena.

At last Ariadne Trevelyan broke her silence.

'You don't have to go,' she said to her sister, 'unless they are arresting you.'

'I am quite prepared to do that,' Sinclair assured them. 'Indeed I suspect it will come to that and if it does you will of course be cautioned and will be entitled to representation.'

'I shall arrange for our solicitor to be present at any further interview, regardless of whether you are arrested,' Ariadne assured her sister.

That really was the end of our involvement in the case until it went to trial and Selena Trevelyan was found guilty of attempted murder. Both Hugo and I were of course summoned as witnesses for the prosecution, as was her accomplice who turned Queen's Evidence in return for partial immunity. Evidence was adduced that Selena was her sister's sole heir. Ariadne Trevelyan refused to testify against her sister but the Crown Prosecutor decided, rightly as it turned out, that the case was strong enough without her evidence and made no effort to compel her to give it. She was nevertheless present and seemingly unmoved throughout, and continues to this day, I have heard, to seek grounds for her sister to appeal although that seems a hopeless endeavour.

Some considerable time later I was again driving through Northumberland and met Hugo for a bar lunch at The Hairy Lemon in Alnwick's Narrowgate. We fell to discussing The Enigma of the Speeding Toadstool.

'It was an imaginative crime,' I opined. 'Pity it had such a banal and sordid motive.'

Hugo looked unusually pensive.

'And such a waste of talent,' he replied. 'In all senses of the noun,' he added grinning. It seemed clear to me that he had been pondering the prolonged sentence of incarceration visited on the younger sister but it turned out that was only part of his regret.

'If only Miss Ariadne Trevelyan applied her financial and mental resources to more worthwhile enterprises than fairies and the vain defence of her obviously guilty sister she could make a considerable contribution to the world.'

'I daresay you are right,' I commented, 'but the viability of civilised society depends on its plurality and it's as well to remember that the freedom to espouse apparently madcap beliefs and the pursuit of seemingly lost causes do on occasion reap unexpected benefits without which we should all be the poorer.'

Hugo smiled.

'I see you are a doctor of not just natural philosophy but of social philosophy too.'

'Heaven forfend!' I shuddered theatrically as I deliberately uttered the archaism.

Enigma of the Image

I'm not sure whether this is a story or a swindle. It is an account of a series of events which made me think deeply about a number of disparate matters. If you can spare the time to read it you may judge for yourself.

Whitechapel has a reputation for lawlessness and yet almost all its inhabitants are no more nor less so than those in other parts of London, or indeed of Britain. Like other urban areas it also has its share of the amenities of civilisation, among them being the prestigious Whitechapel Art Gallery and the adjacent but often under-valued public library. Less well-known is Grodzinski's Gallery and it was thither that I made my way one sunny afternoon feeling in need of an escape from the undoubtedly also civilised but rather intro-verted academic environment of the college in which I work and spend most of my days.

I emerged from the London Underground next to the library and walked along Whitechapel High Street, which I crossed with some difficulty, and then turned into Rope Passage, an old and narrow street leading southward towards the river. Not far along it I came to the entrance to Grodzinski's.

I climbed the narrow stairs and pushed open the door at their top which let me into a medium sized room whose walls displayed a number of very large paintings, except for the wall on the street side of the building which was devoid of art, unless one were to regard as such the two very big windows which were bright with the blue sky of summer. Apparently staring through one of these was a small dumpy man who appeared against the brightness as not much more than a silhouette.

Hearing the door sigh shut, the figure turned revealing it was Lionel Grodzinski, the younger brother being as usual at Whitechapel, his elder sibling presumably being at their Bond Street main gallery. His face lit up with a welcoming smile.

'Ah, Dr Dunkley, greetings! It is too long since you last paid a visit to my tiny but blessed emporium.' He laughed and I smiled in return.

'I come only when I am thirsty for the treasures you display, never as the result of an ordered routine.'

'Ah, ever the silver tongue,' he rejoined. 'Had you been a painter you would not have prospered in this present age of coarse and brutal taste. But you are in for a rich reward today. Since your last visit I have acquired an unusual and exceptionally fine item for your admiration. I leave you to discover it for yourself.' He gestured expansively towards the interior of the gallery.

It is a small establishment and there is never any need to race round for fear of not having time to see everything so, as usual, I viewed the exhibits methodically. Most I had of course seen before. Those that were new I gave a chance to speak to me. As always there were those that remained mute or chattered in a language I didn't know but since the Grodzinski brothers hardly ever allowed anything devoid of all merit to sully their walls I always made an effort to understand. The one occasion when I was moved to protest that a painting seemed to me complete rubbish, Lionel agreed and his explanation led to the enigma of *The Expensive Daub*! So I always did the artists the courtesy of assuming that any lack of communication between us was my fault and not theirs.

It was in the largest of the four rooms that I encountered what I had no doubt was the exhibit Lionel meant. The brothers did not display much sculpture in their East End gallery because of its constricted space, so what it did make room for was almost always outstanding.

I saw it from the doorway.

It dominated the room, not by its scale which was only a little more than lifesize, but by its sheer presence.

It was a human figure cast in bronze, a man, his attitude one of surprise, of being arrested by something in the act of leaning forward and as I moved closer I saw that the expression on the face too was one of surprise. One of his hands was stretched forward and half-clenched as though holding something, like a paint brush, that is an artist's brush and I could readily imagine that he was in fact leaning towards a canvas on an easel, that his surprise was a realisation of where the next brush stroke should go.

'It's an image of the painter Kyril Grimkin by his brother Gifford,' murmured Grodzinski. I'd been so absorbed in contemplation of the work that I had not noticed his entry. He had a quiet tread in any case, presumably so as not to startle possible customers.

I knew something of the biographies of the Grimkin twins, Kyril and Gifford. Born in Ince-in-Makersfield, they studied at Manchester School of Art, where L S Lowry once attended classes. They briefly went their separate ways after that, Kyril to Paris to study painting and Gifford to Florence for sculpture, but some years later they were back in Britain in time to be minor participants in the tail-end of Brit-art. They bought or rented studio space together in Spitalfields.

Kyril painted in fits and starts but

intensely, catching passing but lucrative fads, selling well but briefly as fashions changed. Gifford was a slower worker, but perhaps with sculpture that is inevitable. They were nowhere near the forefront of their generation but Gifford especially seemed to be establishing a solid reputation.

Kyril married, a Linda Bedelgart, which stabilised his finances because she had a steady job, something to do with banking, not the greedy risky kind but the respectable everyday custodianship of wealth, the mechanics of money.

'I haven't seen anything much in the way of new work from them lately,' I said, as that realisation dawned on me. Lionel Grodzinski smiled his slightly crooked smile.

'Were I a lecturer and you one of my students I should be constrained to suggest you had not been paying attention,' he said in his prolix fashion, 'but given our actual circumstances I would not venture to be so impertinent; yet I am surprised if you are unaware what has been happening with the pair of them over the last two years.'

I confessed I'd heard nothing noteworthy, and suppressed a smile as I reflected that some of my students seemed to be in the same situation during my lectures.

'I think Kyril's marriage broke up,' related Lionel. 'Anyway he returned to sharing the flat the two brothers owned above their studio in Spitalfields, but his productivity, always spasmodic, slumped. Fortunately for the pair of them Gifford's output remained fairly constant and prices for his work rose steadily so that between them they were able to get by. Then Kyril effectively disappeared. According to Gifford he'd gone abroad and was just travelling aimlessly. At first, said Gifford, he received occasional postcards from his brother, but for the last year or so there's been no word from him.

'Although Gifford's sculpture had generally been more highly regarded than Kyril's painting, especially by the critics, there had always been a small number of loyal collectors of his canvasses and when it dawned on them that the supply had dried up, those still unsold in one of the few galleries like us who dealt in them were eagerly snapped up and prices commanded by the odd one or two that subsequently were resold, rose accordingly.

'Gifford still came into the gallery occasionally to bring in the odd piece of new work for sale, small but certainly not trifling figurines, but he seemed to have lost impetus. Never a fast worker, he appeared to have slowed almost to a halt. Eventually he confided in me that he was very worried by Kyril's long silence and feared some illness or accident had befallen him. It was sapping his own will to work.'

'He must have recovered,' I observed when Grodzinski at last fell silent. I gestured towards the bronze. 'I realise I am a poor and inattentive student of art but this strikes me as a very fine piece.' Grodzinski nodded vigorously.

'It is indeed. I was very surprised when it arrived. A white van drew up outside the gallery one afternoon, completely blocking the passage. When I went down to see what was happening, Gifford and another man, whom I assumed was the driver were carefully unloading a stretcher from the back of the van. On it was a large object carefully wrapped in blankets, looking for all the world like a body! With some help from me, they manoeuvred it up the stairs and into the gallery. The driver left immediately in response to impatient hooting outside. I watched while Grimkin removed the wrappings and revealed this!'

Lionel stood gazing at the statue.

'Did Gifford actually say it was a portrait of his brother?' I asked as a thought occurred to me.

'Well no,' admitted Lionel, 'but it's obvious from the face and the hand which clearly would be grasping a brush.'

'Or a chisel,' I suggested. 'Might it not be Gifford himself?'

Lionel was silent for a minute or two.

'Ye-es,' he said uncertainly. He took a step forward and examined the hand carefully. 'You could be right,' he conceded. He grinned. 'I withdraw my earlier criticism of inattention! It could be Kyril or Gifford, portrait or self-portrait.'

Abruptly I realised that time was

passing. Glancing at my watch I saw I would have to leave to get back to College in time to take a tutorial. I murmured a muted thanks and farewell and left Lionel contemplating the figure.

The following week Hugo Lacklan was in London for a symposium. We met up one evening and I told him of the impression Gifford Grimkin's new work had made on me and, as I'd expected he said he'd like to see it too. On the Wednesday afternoon, Hugo's symposium was over and I was free of laboratory classes and had no meetings to attend so we met in Whitechapel Library and ambled along to Grodzinski's Gallery.

As I'd anticipated, Hugo was as impressed as I was by the image. He questioned Lionel closely but learnt not much more about it than the gallery owner had told me previously.

'No,' the latter admitted, 'I don't know if it's a recent work. I did get the impression though, that it had been completed some time ago and had been languishing in Grimkin's studio. Why he should suddenly have decided now was the time to exhibit it I don't know.'

'You've put no price on it yet?' queried Hugo.

'No, it's not for sale!' There was a hint of exasperation in Grodzinski's answer, no doubt the frustration of the salesman! 'Gifford insisted on that. He wants people to be able to see it but doesn't want to part with it — anybody would think I'm running a museum here! What's more he specified that it should be in the East End gallery and not the Bond Street one, though it could be displayed to much better advantage there because of the space we have in the West End gallery. It's so that he can come and see it easily himself — not that he's been in since he delivered it. It's almost as though he was grieving for his brother, as if he were not just travelling abroad but, well travelling in the realms of the dead, as though this were a burial ground and that his tombstone!'

I found this a chilling observation. The idea pointed in a number of alarming possible directions. There was silence in the gallery as though we were each exploring our own imagined pathways.

A clatter of shoes and a babble of voices from the stairwell shook us free of our introspection. It sounded as though a horde of children was about to invade the gallery. In fact only three burst into the room but they were enough to monopolise Grodzinski's attention. Despite his oft repeated assertion that one of the main reasons for maintaining a gallery in the East End was to give local young people the chance to familiarise themselves with art, he watched these new visitors with all the vigilance a sweet shop proprietor might have done! Of course he wasn't concerned that they might steal any of the exhibits, but he clearly thought inadvertent damage was a distinct possibility. However my own observation suggested they really were interested in the paintings and they soon quietened down, apart from the occasional hoot of derision or knowing snigger. It seemed to me they were indeed discerning critics and budding connoisseurs! Hugo and I left Lionel to his guardianship and slipped away, I to College, Hugo to his flat I assumed.

It must have been a few weeks later that I had to travel across London early one Thursday afternoon to a meeting at Senate House and I went by underground. I'd already read the papers for the meeting and the agenda confirmed my fears that it was likely to be a tedious one, wrangling about standardising admissions criteria, and I'd forgotten to bring anything else with me to read so an abandoned copy of the early edition of the evening paper was irresistible. I picked it up and unfolded it at the front page to be confronted by a quarter page photograph of the statue of Kyril Grimkin in Grodzinski's Gallery, only it wasn't in the gallery but in the centre of a small square surrounded by city buildings. There were people in the picture, mostly caught simply hurrying by but two were staring at the statue with faintly puzzled expressions.

Beneath the photograph was the highly unoriginal truncated caption 'Now you see it . . . ', and below that in smaller type in parenthesis (*Turn to page 5*). I did so and was not at all surprised to see an almost identical shot but without the statue, and with the caption ' . . . now you don't.' The two photos had date and time stamps on them purporting to show that they were taken at 16.35 and 16.45 the previous Monday. The story line did little more than summarise the pictures with the additional note that the photographs had been sent in to the paper by a reader and that careful examination by the paper's experts (I smiled to myself) had found no evidence of fakery.

For most readers no doubt the paired pictures would generate no more than a passing curiosity and slight amusement, but for me they were bewildering. I puzzled over them through the most tedious discussions at the meeting and broke my journey back to College at the gallery. Lionel was sitting at the small table in the vestibule of the gallery with a copy of the evening paper in front of him.

'I don't understand it at all,' he said without so much as a greeting. He shook his head in frustration.

'Has Grimkin been exhibiting the statue in that square?' I asked.

'No, no. I'm sure that statue hasn't left

153

the gallery, not since it arrived. The statue must have been photographed before Grimkin brought it here, either in the square and these dates on the photographs in the paper being faked somehow, or a photo taken of the square and the image of the statue inserted by some technical trickery. You can't really believe anything you see these days. I suppose he might possibly have made another casting of the statue from the mould and be ferrying that around the City.'

'Perhaps. I can't really see the point though. The effort involved in any such fraud would be considerable.'

'Publicity,' stated Grodzinski succinctly.

I began to think he might be right over the next few weeks as more pictures appeared in the papers of the bronze sculpture of Kyril Grimkin in a variety of locations on the periphery of the City of London, and even a short clip of film on the regional television news, although unfortunately it didn't capture the image either arriving or departing or moving in any way at all! If publicity was the aim it certainly succeeded at least for a while. A number of the news stories mentioned that the statue was at present exhibited in Grodzinski's Gallery and I imagined that would up the visitor numbers at the gallery appreciably, and indeed Lionel himself said as much in a brief interview by a BBC journalist screened another night. Attempts were made to interview Gifford Grimkin as well and their lack of success was reported as 'The artist was unavailable for comment' as though he were a government minister responsible for the latest privatisation fiasco or outrage!

I was particularly busy at College and a couple of months slipped by before I revisited the gallery, and then only because Hugo was again in town and, planning to go himself, he persuaded me I could spare the time. The effusiveness of Lionel's greeting startled me.

'Ah I am so glad you're here!' He had a strained look about his face and seemed too to have lost weight. 'I am driven almost to distraction!'

'What on earth is the matter?'

Grodzinski urged us, almost drove us into the larger room, the one housing the statue of Kyril Grimkin. He jabbed his finger at the bronze.

'Supposing he's in there!' he hissed in a sibilant whisper.

The horror of the idea had an awful seductiveness which we all contemplated in silence for some minutes. Hugo broke the mood with a determined briskness.

'There are three possible responses. Firstly, ignore the possibility as too fantastic to be true . . . ' Grodzinski interrupted with a violent shake of his head.

'No! Already I can't sleep at night for thinking of it. I can hardly bear to come into the gallery in the morning to face it and the thought that I might encounter it somewhere else at any time is terrifying.'

'The second,' went on Hugo 'is to establish Kyril's actual present whereabouts and so disprove the suggestion. I have indeed been trying to do that over the last two months but in vain. I have contacted people I know in various parts of the world but have discovered nothing positive. It's unsatisfactory I know but the third approach also has its problems — we could look inside the statue.'

'No!' protested Grodzinski once again. 'It's a work of art; we mustn't damage it.'

Lionel was clearly distraught at the suggestions offered by Hugo, looking tense, drawn and apprehensive. It grieved me to see him so agitated and I was surprised by how much this pained me. I realised with a sudden insight that he was no longer just an interesting and slightly amusing character that I knew, but that over the years he'd become a friend, someone I cared about. I was brought up sharp by the realisation that I didn't actually have many true friends outside College and that even there the number of colleagues whom I would consider close friends was small. The real meaning of the banal admonition 'You should get out more!' abruptly struck home and I understood that since Helen's death I had indeed turned unhealthily inward. I had many acquaintances, some of them like Lionel I had known for years and I would have listed him along with them but I now revised that judgement. I valued the relationship I had with him and felt a desire to relieve his distress if I could.

Suddenly Lionel brightened, interrupting my rather morbid introspection.

'Ah, do you mean we could X-ray it?' he asked. Both Hugo and I shook our heads, but Hugo left it to me to explain.

'X-rays can't penetrate bronze. The same goes for other scanning techniques. Gamma radiation of short enough wavelength would penetrate but then detection and interpretation is a problem; neutron scanning might theoretically be effective but the equipment is far too cumbersome to be portable and so the bronze effectively conceals whatever is within from non-invasive examination.' I paused.

'What would be feasible, and what Hugo also has in mind I imagine, is that we could drill a tiny hole in the figure, somewhere that it won't normally be visible, like the sole of the foot, and insert an optical fibre to illuminate the cavity within and another to record what is revealed — essentially a miniature television camera.' Hugo nodded.

'You have one of those things?'

'No, but I can borrow one from a colleague,' answered Hugo confidently.

On Sunday afternoon, just over a week later, Hugo and I had arranged to meet at Grodzinski's. I'd spent the morning in the department at College catching up on work but left in time to walk down the Mile End Road to the vicinity of the gallery — I needed the exercise and it was a fine day. As luck would have it, when I was nearly at my destination I espied Hugo approaching from the other direction, presumably from Aldgate East underground station. I was surprised to see he had someone with him and even more surprised when I saw it was Arnold Henderson, the chief technician from the College workshop. They were both carrying canvas bags that looked heavy. I waited at the pedestrian crossing since we would need to go over the road. When they reached me we greeted each other.

'Didn't expect to see you Arnold.'

'Didn't expect to be here! My brother Tommy is Chief Tech in the Department of Anthropology at the Northern Cities Metropolitan University. He rang me a couple of nights ago, said Dr Lacklan wanted to borrow a portable high

159

precision drill from the workshop there and suggested it'd be more convenient if he borrowed one from the workshop here, seeing as how he knew you were involved and our College is so much closer to where it's needed.'

'And did he suggest you might lend us a hand as well as the drill?'

Arnold grinned.

'No, but I've heard a bit from Tommy about Dr Lacklan and I thought it'd be best for the drill if I came along too.'

'You shouldn't believe everything people say about me,' said Hugo. 'Universities are as notorious as the Women's Institute for being hotbeds of gossip.'

'Oh, neither Tommy nor I believe everything we hear; just the discreditable bits!'

By this time we had, fortunately, reached the gallery. Lionel was standing inside the glass door with its neat 'Closed' sign. Evidently he had been on the lookout for us and he welcomed us in.

We trooped upstairs to the room with the bronze in it. We carefully laid it down on its back on a blanket Lionel had already spread ready. He'd also rigged up a number of spot lights to give us plenty of illumination. Arnold unpacked his drill, inserted a fine metal bit and plugging it in, set to work. I imagine the others felt the same tense expectancy as I did myself. No one spoke, indeed the deathly silence was broken only by the whine of the drill As it connected with the sole of the figure's foot it sounded like a particularly excruciating dental drill, enough to set all our teeth on edge! Arnold squirted a fluid from an oil can onto it to cool it. A small pile of turnings accumulated below. Fortunately it wasn't too long before it slid easily forward indicating it was through into a cavity or at any rate something much softer. Arnold eased it out, cut the power, and laid the drill aside. He cleaned the hole with a pipe cleaner.

Hugo took an odd sort of camera from his bag and gently inserted an optical fibre into the hole. There were a few tense moments as it seemed to snag on something and Hugo jiggled it carefully and then it moved forward freely and we all breathed sighs of relief. I assumed the others, like me, interpreted that to mean the interior was empty.

The camera screen was small and we had to take it in turns to view inside. When it was my own I found it was like gazing into a huge cavern with side galleries full of mysterious shadows. My eyes followed the moving viewpoint of the camera as Hugo guided the optical fibre over the inner surface and I saw it was far from smooth.

Tensions had dissipated swiftly. Lionel was jubilant.

'Thank you my friends,' he said. 'Let's have a drink to celebrate!' He dived into his office and re-emerged with a clutch of glasses and a bottle of what I saw was Wodka Luksusowa, a Polish vodka which is made from potatoes and is strong stuff! We were all soon laughing immoderately at our own former credulous apprehension. When the bottle was empty, Lionel said:

'Now food! I would like to take you all out to dinner!' He was too determined to take our demurrals seriously and insisted. He said he'd been unable to eat properly for the last few days because of worry about the statue so he was really hungry and he would enjoy eating so much more in company. Of course he took us to a Polish restaurant and we drank a Polish wine of some potency. The inevitable result of so much celebrating was that we all felt somewhat removed from the world when we left the restaurant. We headed back to Aldgate East station in high spirits, then Lionel went on to the gallery, Arnold headed off on the District Line to Plaistow where he lived with his mother and Hugo got a westbound Metropolitan line train to the Barbican where his town flat is.

I travelled with Arnold as far as the station for College, an amusing journey as the vodka and the wine encouraged him to be more forthcoming on the subject of Hugo than he might otherwise have been, and had likewise made me more receptive to his indiscretions than I might normally have considered proper. Perhaps fortunately for all three of us although I remember being excessively amused, I can't recall any of the actual stories his brother had told him and which he recounted.

When I reached my office I made myself some coffee and relaxed into the old easy chair I had hung onto despite its incongruous appearance in what is in fact a small laboratory as well as an office (the building was put up in more spacious days!). I fell into a doze despite the coffee and when I woke I had sobered up sufficiently to realize that I wasn't really sober enough to drive! So I went home to my cottage in the Chilterns by public transport, still feeling mellow enough not to get impatient at the time it took.

As a consequence I had to commute back to College by train on Monday morning and was not feeling at all mellow by then. When the underground train I was in stopped two stations before the one for College, a group of students boarded it and I was roused from semi-doze by a cheerful hail in a voice rather too penetrating for my condition.

'Good morning Dr Dunkley! Heavy weekend?'

I opened my eyes and recognised among the students who had sat down opposite me a number who were presumably bound for my nine o'clock lecture. They were grinning.

'Yes thank you,' was the best reply I could manage.

When I stepped into the lecture theatre it was obvious to me that the undergraduates on the train had shared their encounter with a fair number of their fellows. I think I gave my lecture competently and once I'd got into my stride the grins were soon replaced by furrowed brows and what I hoped was earnest concentration.

To my regret, after giving three lectures in the morning I also had a laboratory supervision all afternoon. However about four the lab phone rang. It was Hugo.

'How are you?' he asked, although I suspected there was more amusement than solicitude in his enquiry.

'Busy,' I answered shortly. 'A lab class of forty students to supervise.' I relented slightly. 'I do have two competent postgraduate demonstrators this term, so unless there's a big fire or explosion I should be able to spare you a few minutes! Where are you phoning from?'

'Kings Cross. I'm getting a late

afternoon train back north. I just wanted to say that although yesterday's investigation may have done enough to lay the ghost haunting Grodzinski, it hasn't actually thrown any light on the reason for Kyril's long absence nor on his present whereabouts. Still, I don't see what more we can do for the moment. I think we'll just have to await further developments.'

'What makes you think there will be any?'

'Call it anthropologist's instinct!'

'I call it infernal curiosity!'

Hugo chuckled.

'I just think it might be worth you popping into the gallery a bit more frequently than of late to keep an eye out, seeing as you are practically on the spot.'

I sighed in exasperation.

'Of course I'd like nothing better than to have the time to visit galleries three or four days a week Hugo, but this term is an extremely busy one.'

'I know. Same for me. Still, Lionel might offer you a tot of that Polish vodka, now he knows you like it!' He rang off!

In fact although I was especially grumpy that Monday after the Sunday before, I was as intrigued as Hugo by the Grimkin twins, as well as still unsettled by that glimpse I'd had of the sparseness of my own inner life. These factors were perhaps partly responsible for me paying the gallery another visit early in the next week.

Lionel was in a tranquil mood in contrast to myself. There was nothing new to see and even reacquainting myself with some of the paintings I particularly liked didn't soothe my restlessness. I stood for a while in front of the one remaining painting by Kyril Grimkin as yet unsold by Grodzinski. It seemed to me he must be reluctant to see it go since the asking price was much higher than a Grimkin was likely to fetch even given their current scarcity. Where, I wondered, was the painter? If he were to return, would he resume painting? Perhaps he'd come back dragging behind him a wagon loaded with canvases executed during his self-exile. I smiled at the fancifulness of the image this thought conjured up. If he did paint again would it be more in his established style or would the break have given rise to something radically different?

'Don't tell me you want to buy it?'

I was so absorbed that I hadn't noticed Lionel come into the room. I smiled.

'Wanting and being able are kept firmly asunder by the price. It is out of my world as well you know.'

'Beyond the established range for a Grimkin as well I hope. I'd be sorry to see it go. So you and anyone else who appreciates it can come and enjoy it whenever they like, at no cost to themselves and without distraction. Much better than it being unseen in the private hoard of some collector.'

'Whenever we have the time,' I contradicted. I glanced at my watch. 'I'd better get back to College.' I took a notepad and pencil from my pocket and carefully inscribed my College direct line number on it.

'If there are any further developments in the Grimkin saga will you give me a ring?' I asked.

'Of course, delighted to. Both you and

Hugo are no doubt as intrigued by the mystery surrounding Kyril Grimkin's disappearance as you are interested in seeing more of his work,' he teased. I nodded.

'Of course. Aren't you?' His expression turned sombre.

'I'm not sure I want to know what's happened to him. I haven't forgotten how I felt when I was afraid he might be entombed in his own image.'

As I walked back to the station along Whitechapel High Street, Billy Bragg's 'Highway to the Sea', I felt disturbed by Lionel's phrase 'entombed in his own image'. Thinking of people I knew, some of them might be so-described, myself included perhaps, our lives sealed within the limits we set for ourselves, our routines and obligations, the personae we tried to project, apparently unable to break out and seek something more fulfilling.

Another thought intruded out of the blue and caused me to smile: the business of the lecture after the Sunday investigation of the statue and the subsequent

169

celebration had just as likely enhanced rather than impaired my own image in the eyes of some at least of the students. But that led me to think about personal images in general. What after all is any image but the product of our own or another person's imagining? So it seemed to me that there are two types of personal image: the image a person constructs for themselves — in which they may hope to reveal or conversely to conceal the truth of what they are or strive to be; and the image of them perceived by others. Of course no one sees things or people in exactly the same way so in speaking of a person's image it must be recognised that there are actually a multiplicity of images, although most of them will have a common core of properties.

A week or so later I was returning to my office from the College library where I'd been checking some primary sources for a review I was writing, having found, as is worryingly all too often the case, that the original papers didn't say quite what those who cited them claimed they did. It suddenly occurred to me that in the matter of the brothers Grimkin, checking the authenticity of the 'commonly known facts' about them was something Hugo and I had neglected to do. The circumstances of their earlier years were just what we'd read somewhere and I confess I couldn't even remember where. Some of it was probably what Lionel had related. If matters were even slightly different from 'common knowledge' we might be looking at the present situation in quite the wrong way. Even if what we thought we knew was correct it was still very meagre. If we *knew* more perhaps we would *understand* all.

When I finally made telephone contact with Hugo I put this point to him and he concurred.

'No doubt you are too busy to undertake field work at the moment,' he concluded, 'but I've to give a lecture in Manchester next week. If I stay that side of the Pennines for a couple of days instead of coming straight back to the North East I can probably fit in a bit of investigating in Ince into their early years and see if it reveals anything.'

'Where the Dickens is Ince anyway?' I asked.

'Wrong author!' said Hugo. 'Not Dickens but Orwell. It's a suburb of Wigan now, though it was once a separate village.'

At the end of the following week Hugo rang to say he'd be passing through London on the morrow and could we meet for lunch in an Italian restaurant we both knew in a quiet street near Angel Islington so he could tell me what he'd discovered, an arrangement I readily accepted.

'Your suggestion may have borne some sort of fruit,' he said. 'I spoke to a friend of a friend at the School of Art in Manchester and he had a look at the record of the Grimkin twins' time there. The only slightly relevant detail he could retail was that they'd collaborated on an installation project. The most helpful piece of information he gave was their address in Ince at the time they applied for admission. I went along to have a look and as I stood outside the nineteenth century terraced cottage I saw an elderly woman peering back at me round the edge of her curtain, so I knocked. Who better to ask about sons than their mother if that's who she should prove to be. Then I reflected, probably lots of people!'

At this point I distinctly remember thinking: he's really spinning this out!

'In the event, however the woman wasn't Mrs Grimkin and told me that they had in fact bought the house from a couple called Hardcastle but she seemed to remember that Grimkin was a name on the deeds from further back. 'Ask Mrs Farmer next door,' she concluded, pointing to the left, 'she's been here forever,' she advised.'

'So I said thanks and goodbye and went next door. 'Her next door' was actually a 'Miss' and older still but as soon as I mentioned Kyril and Gifford her face lit up and she said yes of course she remembered them well and asked me in. Unsurprisingly she said she was just about to make herself a cup of tea and would I like one and I naturally said yes as I find it's always easier to elicit information over a cup of tea! She pointed to a photograph on the mantel piece, of two small boys who looked exactly alike, and said she'd forgotten now which one was which and wasn't that awful. I let her ramble on because, to be honest, I was quite glad to sit down for a bit and the room was warm and the tea was hot and strong and she'd brought in a plate of home-made biscuits.'

At this point in his monologue Hugo sounded as though the recollection of a drowsy interview was about to send him into a remembered sleep so I interrupted him.

'I thought you were intending just to pass through London, not take root here. I have a tutorial to give this afternoon, so could you save the local colour for the memoirs I have no doubt you intend to write one day and just apprise me of any facts that emerged?'

'Well yes, if you really are in such a hurry. I thought you might be glad of some authentic detail in case we ever get to the bottom of this matter and you want to write it up. As for my memoirs I rather hoped you might ghost those for me, providing you give me ample opportunity to cut out your snide asides of course.

Very well then, the edited version of the interview is that Miss Farmer's memory of the twins was quite detailed. As she lived alone and had no close kin left, the two boys were an important source of human interest for her.

'She said she never could tell them apart and she was sure they took advantage of their identical appearance to play tricks not just on her but others too. Up to a certain age their mother dressed them identically and appeared to treat them as interchangeable. Later she did vary their outfits but it didn't help a lot. You know how even with non-identical twins if you are only acquainted with them casually it can be hard to remember which name goes with which face, Miss Farmer told me. Even when they went to college and dressed consistently differently, one even growing a beard, she'd remember for a day or two after seeing them, which one it was who had the beard but after a while she was confused again.

'I know I've gone on a bit about this confusion but I feel it may be significant even now in some way, as if those tricks they played foreshadowed something that was to come later, like an artist's preliminary sketches for a future master work. Miss Farmer related one other thing I felt particularly suggestive. Both their mother and father fell ill at the same time — flu she thought it was but it dragged on and on — and the boys took it in turns to come home every few days. They were still in their one bearded and one clean-shaven period so she knew they took it in turns. They always popped in to see her too and to ask how their Mum and Dad seemed to her to be managing as they knew she looked in every day to see if they needed anything doing urgently. Mrs Grimkin was able to cook basic meals and Mr Grimkin could do snacks so they coped but just couldn't shake off the malaise.'

I think at this juncture I began to get restive again, and Hugo came quickly to the point.

'On one of the last occasions he came, Kyril was accompanied by a very pretty girl whom he introduced to Miss Farmer as Linda. The girl asked if she might remain with Miss Farmer while Kyril visited his parents as she was peculiarly susceptible to viral infections. The following week Gifford brought Linda with him. And the strange thing was he introduced them just as though Kyril hadn't already done so! Gifford seemed quite natural but Miss Farmer thought there was something a bit odd, almost sly, about the girl's smile. She had the impression that Linda was almost daring Miss Farmer to say she remembered her from the previous visit. It put Miss Farmer in a bit of a flutter, not knowing what to say or what the consequences might be if she spoke up, so in the end she kept quiet. Once again the girl stayed with Miss Farmer while Gifford went next door. Miss Farmer said she was a very pleasant girl otherwise and she would have enjoyed their conversation if it were not for the peculiar circumstances. It had worried her for quite a while afterwards though.'

Hugo paused and looked at me as though inviting comment.

'That's a bit of facer,' I said rather lamely.

'It suggests a possible motive don't you think? For one brother to do away with the other? I know Linda is a common name but if the Linda of their student days was the same Linda Kyril married, maybe his disappearance really is permanent. Gifford might have killed Kyril so he could have Linda, or Kyril might have murdered Gifford out of jealously and then taken on his identity. Either way it might account for the erratic nature of the twins output, if one was having to adjust to an unfamiliar medium.'

'The identification seems a bit speculative, but if what you say is true, Linda must have been a party to the act or at least know about it.' Hugo nodded.

'If Miss Farmer's impression of Linda's slyness was valid and if she is indeed the same Linda then that might be all of a piece with her character.' After a moment's reflection he resumed.

'I didn't learn much more. Miss Farmer said when the boys graduated their mother gave her photographs of each of them in their graduation robes. Miss

Farmer pointed to them, one on each side of the mantel piece, although I had naturally already noticed them. They looked indistinguishable. Of course their academic dress was the same as they'd been awarded the same degree, and their features remained identical but their expression was also exactly the same, a sort of sardonic smile.'

'I suppose the two prints weren't made from a photograph of just one of the twins — to save on cost?' I suggested, only half in jest. Hugo shrugged.

'I wouldn't put it past them, though not necessarily to save money but simply as a prank. I've just no idea. Come to think of it, on the two visits Linda made to Miss Farmer she could quite well have been accompanied by the same twin, if he'd shaved off the beard in the interim or indeed had attached a false one, depending in which order the visits occurred.'

It was barely a week later that Lionel's call reached me sitting at my desk in my office, interrupting me in a bout of vacant gazing through the window at the seemingly endless procession of white summer clouds across the blue.

'Something odd,' he said excitedly. 'Gifford has brought in some new work. It's, um, unexpected.'

'In what way?'

'I can't describe it adequately. You'll have to see it for yourself.'

I glanced at my watch and then, instead of protesting I was busy as I usually did, I admitted frankly to myself that I just wasn't managing to concentrate on the problem with which I was meant to be wrestling, and decided I might as well give up for the afternoon. I appeased my conscience by telling myself I might then be able to conclude the work this evening.

'I'll come now.'

I walked, hoping to refresh my brain, so it was some time before I arrived at the gallery after all.

'Go and look,' directed Grodzinski, without preamble, 'and then tell me what you think.'

There were a few other people in the gallery — a couple who looked like students, an elderly man with a vacant expression, and a middle-aged woman with a sad face.

Of course the figure of Kyril — or perhaps Gifford — Grimkin was still there and still commanding attention, dominating the room in which it stood, but now sharing it with a new exhibit — or perhaps a dozen new exhibits; it depended how you viewed what was there. At first I saw them as individual pieces but then they seemed to come together as a whole, perhaps even drawing in the figure of Kyril since they were at the end of the room at which the statue appeared to be gazing. He might just have stood back from them to judge their effect.

There were four small pottery pieces, each on its own three foot high plinth. They were realist but also in a way abstract. At first glance they might be thought of as distorted jugs, tall rather elegant vessels reminiscent of vases but each of them had a handle of sorts. They reminded me of the illustrations you see in popularisations of mathematical ideas, in this case attempts to represent a Klein bottle, the single-surfaced four-dimensional analogue of the Moebius strip.

They were arranged in a row across the

width of the room and each one was strongly lit by a floor level light angled upwards, so each 'bottle' threw a shadow on the wall behind, four very different shadows due to the angle at which each vessel was set to the plane so that the shadows suggested that each bottle was different, and concealed the fact that they actually were all the same shape. It was as if the group of pots together with their shadows reminded the viewer that what we think of as the real world was merely a shadow of it.

But that was not all! Behind each bottle hung a painting just above the shadows thrown on the wall. Each picture was a representation of the bottle before it in an elegantly restrained cubist mode reminiscent of Juan Gris, showing all possible views including the inside. The pottery of course was opaque, but the paintings attempted to render the vessels transparent — to show in some way how they appeared 'within'.

The area of the wall encompassing the shadows and canvases was 'framed' by four strips of moulded wood suggestive of a picture frame as though to emphasise the integrity of the installation.

There was room on the wall to one side of the enclosing wood for a small white card on which was printed the title of the work: Klein's Cavern, and the identity of the artist: Grimkin.

I was stunned.

'You see why I described it as unexpected?' asked a voice which I seemed to be hearing as though from a remote place. It startled me from my contemplation.

'Yes indeed it is, in several different ways,' I answered Grodzinski slowly. 'I think, but remember my speciality is chemistry not topology and I've no real grasp of more than three dimensions, but what I think is that the artist is trapped in the cave's three dimensions and can see only the shadows of four dimensional realities from which he tries to visualise their true nature and then attempt to represent it in two dimensional paintings of three dimensional representations of the imagined four dimensional manifolds.'

'You are making my head spin,' complained Lionel. 'Can you perhaps explain your explanation?' I grinned sympathetically.

'Hugo needs to see this,' I went on with sudden decisiveness, incidentally avoiding his plea.

'There's something else you should see,' continued Lionel. 'Nothing to compare with this,' he hastened to say. 'From an artistic point of view not at all unexpected, but given its appearance in conjunction with this, quite surprising.' He drew me into the adjoining room and pointed at a landscape. It was by Kyril Grimkin, not one I'd seen before.

'Gifford said it was in their store room.' Something about the tone of Lionel's voice made me glance at him quizzically.

'You don't believe that?'

Grodzinski looked unhappy.

'If I say no you'll ask me why and I'll have to admit I don't really know. It's just a feeling I have.'

'Based on experience or instinct do you think?'

'Ah,' he smiled. 'A discerning distinction. I have to confess to the latter.'

'Never to be despised,' I assured him,

'though I suspect the latter draws heavily on the former in reality. As the years pass I find myself valuing instinct more and more highly. I suspect it integrates all those clues we don't consciously notice, don't recognise, can't evaluate; sometimes it overtakes and forges ahead of reason.'

'It seems a strange, perhaps even a dangerous, attitude for a scientist to adopt.'

'Ah, but if it is particularly acute it may end up being described by posterity as 'insight'. I suspect many a Nobel prize has in reality been awarded for successful instinct.'

'Even so, there are I think some concrete reasons for my doubt. I *do* think the paint is surprisingly fresh — it hasn't been glazed, did you notice?'

I smiled.

'I tend to look at the picture, not the painting I must admit.'

We stood looking at it for a while.

'Do you suppose Kyril has returned?' I asked presently.

'Perhaps, in a way at any rate. Ach, I'm confused,' he grumbled, throwing up his hands and doing his continental act.

When I got back to College I phoned Hugo. He still refuses to have a mobile or if he has one, to switch it on and my call to his extension went through to Mrs Desai, the departmental secretary. She greeted me warmly.

'He is in somewhere. I'll leave him a message.'

When he rang me back I spoke fairly briefly, I didn't want to colour his first impressions of the installation and tried to confine myself to convincing him that both Lionel and I felt it was significant enough, not only in artistic terms, but in relation to the mystery surrounding the twins, for him to see it as soon as he was able. He said he could be in London the following Wednesday evening.

'I'll stay at the flat,' (his home from home when he's in London — don't ask me how he affords it). 'Will you check with Grodzinski that Thursday will be okay for me to look in?'

'All right,' I answered. 'Anything else? Shall I order the milk and papers for you?'

'Sorry,' laughed Hugo, sounding it not at all. 'It's just that you are on the spot.'

'Yes and it's you that keeps putting me there!'

'Very droll.' He laughed again.

'After all,' I said, 'telecommunications have all but annihilated distances between people, so 'being there' is irrelevant for the purpose of making arrangements.'

'I know, I know. You are right. I am inordinately lazy about such things.'

'In fact,' I said, 'it is much more efficient if you phone Lionel since I don't actually need to be there at all. I've seen it once and still have a vague recollection of it even though it will have been a whole week ago,' I finished sarcastically.

'I give in. I'll let you know the time though, as it would be useful if we were both there if it is as revealing as you say.'

'Of course, I will try to make it. I would in fact like to see it again.'

Hugo did ring me back and said that Lionel had persuaded him that Thursday evening after the gallery was closed to the general public would be best. 'So I'll travel down on Thursday during the day after all. He said we wouldn't get near the installation during opening hours, claims he's over-run with visitors. He admitted he was exaggerating a bit but claimed the amount of interest there'd been in the exhibit since word started to get round was formidable.'

When I looked in on the gallery a few days later I saw for myself that Grodzinski hadn't misled Hugo much. I'd never seen the place so crowded before. Lionel freed himself from a conversation with a rather over-powering woman and sidled over to where I was standing. He rolled his eyes heavenward, or at any rate, at the ceiling.

'Must be good for business,' I tried to console him.

'No one has eyes for anything but the installation, so no one buys anything.' He relented. 'No, that's not quite true. I have sold rather more than usual and I suspect that even when all the fuss dies down people who've come here now for the first time won't all forget the gallery's existence. A small number will come back and may buy work by less prominent, and of course therefore less expensive, but deserving artists. So you are right, it is good but I miss my peace and quiet.'

When finally Hugo saw the installation I could tell he was as impressed as Lionel and I were. He too stared at it for a long time. Then I noticed a change in his attention and I recognised his shift into 'forensic mode',

'Leaving aside the artistic and philosophical questions the work poses,' he began as though speaking either to himself or to a large audience but not specifically to the two of us, 'it's puzzling that it should appear now.'

'It's been a long time since Gifford offered any new work for sale, since he steadfastly refuses to sell the effigy of Kyril, and some time even since he found what he thought was the last of the paintings Kyril completed before he disappeared. Until that is he found that new one he claims to have overlooked previously. So it may be that he is feeling the pecuniary goad.' Although Grodzinski occasionally adopts the fractured English of a recent immigrant, despite being third or fourth generation, he also has a propensity for orotund speech. I have a suspicion that when he indulges in this he is perhaps

189

making fun of Hugo and I as I realise we both have a rather old-fashioned and pedantic diction.

'He must have been working on the installation for some time,' I observed. 'Even if the idea came as a flash of inspiration there's a lot of work involved in the pottery and the painting, especially if Gifford did both. After all, painting isn't his customary medium and so I doubt he has the same facility as Kyril would. And neither the pots nor the canvases are simple pieces despite their apparent modesty.'

'Perhaps after all he did have help,' suggested Hugo.

'Ah, you too wonder if Kyril has returned,' said Lionel. 'I have seen no overt sign of that.'

'Did Gifford ask that the installation be set up in that position?' asked Hugo. Lionel nodded.

'I asked,' went on Hugo, 'because I wonder if there's intended to be a connection between the figure and the display. Is it intended to be in effect a single work?'

'The title card doesn't suggest that to

me,' said Lionel, 'although I confess to being somewhat mystified as to its meaning. Can either of you elucidate?'

'Ah yes,' responded Hugo, 'it is I imagine an allusion to Plato's Cave, a parable the philosopher attributed to his hero Socrates in *The Republic*. In essence it describes a number of prisoners born in a cave and hampered in such a way that they can look at only one wall of it. Behind them is a light source and people passing between the light and the prisoners so that the latter see the people's shadows cast on the wall. They never see any of them directly, only as shadows. All they think they know of the world is what those shadows suggest to them.'

'Yes I remember the story now, but Klein?'

'Felix Klein was a German mathematical physicist,' I said, 'interested in projective geometry. He was intrigued by the Moebius strip which has only one side and only one edge. A Klein bottle has one side but no edges. It exhibits its real nature only in higher dimensions than three so any representation of it in our world, such as these pots, can never be anything more than a shadow of its real shape. Their shadows on the two dimensional surface of the wall are in a sense shadows of shadows.'

'You suggested Grimkin may need to make a sale but there's no price on this newest exhibit,' pointed out Hugo, (unintentionally rescuing me from the quagmire of half understood topology).

'No, Gifford asked me what I reckoned he should ask. Neither of the brothers seems ever to have had an agent and I suppose over the years I've come to act as one unofficially. It's only an informal arrangement but it seems to have worked well. It saves them an agent's fee since I am quite content with the gallery's commission and of course it's as much in my interest as it is in theirs' to get the best price I can. As far as I know they've never offered their work to any other gallery so I assume they too are happy with the arrangement.

'Anyway, he asked what I thought but to be honest I was stumped for an answer. It's such a radical departure for him — or them, whichever it is. I said I'd think it over and I've come to the conclusion that it would be best to put it up for auction. I am going round to the studio to talk to Grimkin about that tomorrow evening.'

'I'd like to see the inside of their studio myself,' mused Hugo. 'Could you make up some excuse for taking me along with you.'

'I suppose so. Has he ever met you?'

'I really don't think so.'

'Then I could say you're a colleague and I want your opinion or something of that sort. I don't want to jeopardise the gallery's relationship with him mind.'

'I won't speak,' Hugo assured him, 'unless I'm spoken to.'

'Hm!' I interjected sceptically.

The following day was of course Friday and about ten that evening Hugo phoned me at the cottage.

'Are you in College tomorrow?' he asked.

'Afraid so,' I sighed. 'Saturdays and Sundays are the only days I've got completely free of teaching this term so I'm usually in on Saturdays to work on my research.'

'I'll pop in about eleven,' he said.

When he arrived we walked over to the senior common room for some coffee.

'Sorry,' I said. 'It's only a machine at the weekends, though personally I find the machine more friendly than the dragon who usually makes it during the week.'

'So what did you discover?' I asked when we'd made ourselves comfortable in armchairs in a corner of the large but mainly empty common room.

'Some surprises,' said Hugo, 'right from the start. The studio and flat the Grimkin brothers own — since I assume they're still their joint property despite the apparent disappearance of Kyril — occupy the third and fourth floors of a building, the lower floors of which are commercial offices. Lionel and I climbed the stairs to the flat and knocked. The door was opened by a strikingly attractive woman. Lionel told me later she was Linda Grimkin — she and Kyril had never bothered to get a divorce. She and Lionel were acquainted from the time when she and Kyril were first married.

She told us Gifford was still in the studio and took us up.

'Whereas the flat was of course divided into a number of rooms, the studio was just one large space apart from a small room cut out of one corner which served as an office and store room for smaller objects. The space was punctuated by a number of columns which gave additional support to the roof which otherwise would have had only the outside walls to rest on. A couple of larger columns looked as though they carried services like electrical wiring and plumbing.

'The space was littered with what you might call art debris — canvases (some bare, some primed, some with works blocked out on them), easels, blocks of stone, piles of paper, jars full of brushes and calligraphy pens, tables, chairs, lamps, mugs, cupboards, shelves, books, chisels, rags, wax. A recording of George Dyson's beautiful violin concerto played softly.

'With all this clutter one thing nevertheless seized my attention and I was not surprised when Lionel told me afterwards that it was the same for him. In the corner diagonally across from the office, resting on a low bench, was what looked like a mummy! Of course that wasn't what it was, at least I don't think so although Lionel fears it might well be. I managed to get a closer look without I hope being too obvious. It was what looked like a body wrapped in bandages and coated with plaster. Lionel said afterwards that it's a technique for producing bronzes of the human form used by artists at least since Aristide Maillol. If it had been used to cast the statue of Kyril, the bandaging would explain the strange markings we saw on the inner surface.'

'Of course,' went on Hugo, 'as soon as we were on our way back to the gallery almost the first thing Grodzinski said was, 'Do you suppose Kyril is in that mummy?''

'Oh no,' I groaned. 'Wasn't he told the fable of the boy who cried 'Wolf!' too often when he was a child?'

Hugo smiled.

'Despite these distractions, Grodzinski

and Grimkin had agreed that the installation should be sold by auction. Lionel said he was sure it would fetch a very good price and he thought Southeby's might be interested in auctioning it. He would get it photographed just as it was in the gallery, for the purposes of illustration. However Linda said she'd get her sister to photograph it once it was finalised. She said her sister had media work training and experience. Lionel didn't argue. As he said afterwards, whoever the auctioneers were they'd want to take their own pictures for their catalogue.

'Grodzinski asked Grimkin if he was working on anything else. Have you noticed how some so-called artists are happy to spend more time talking about how they're busy on this that and the other than actually doing it? Whereas others are reluctant to admit they are working on anything at all? And that it is of course usually the latter who suddenly produce something seemingly out of nowhere while the other lot are still boasting? Grimkin is clearly one of the silent doer tribe. He was non-committal, but looking round the studio there was unmistakable evidence of work in progress in both clay and paint, but mostly of the more abstract styles utilised in Klein's Cavern.'

'Do you think it's all Gifford's work, that he really has taken to painting as well as three dimensional forms, or might Kyril have resurfaced at last?'

'I couldn't decide,' admitted Hugo. 'Lionel did ask Gifford if he'd heard anything from Kyril and Gifford smiled enigmatically and said 'Yes, he talks to me all the time now.' I found his manner distinctly spooky!'

We suddenly realised that time had flown and I decided I wasn't going to settle to anymore work, so I suggested we go and find an early lunch. Hugo agreed. We walked down to Whitechapel, by which time it was no longer going to be an early lunch, but we got a reasonable snack in the cafe over the Whitechapel Gallery. Hugo suggested we waste the rest of the afternoon by calling in at Grodzinski's Gallery.

Lionel was pleased, almost relieved, to see us. He clearly was still fretting about his suspicion that the mummy in the studio contained Kyril. Both Hugo and I tried to reassure him that it was unlikely in the extreme for various practical reasons, but obsessions are hard to reason away. Finally Hugo said:

'I really don't see any easy way of confirming or refuting the possibility. It's not like the statue which, being here in the gallery we could investigate without anyone else knowing. I'm really not prepared to risk breaking into the Grimkin studio in the middle of the night to drill a hole in that mummy!' I was both relieved and slightly surprised to hear Hugo say that — breaking and entering were not unknown to him in the course of explicating one of his enigmas! Lionel saw the force of the argument but was unappeased.

'Look,' said Hugo, 'why don't we ask an expert. Let's lay the whole matter before Sebastian and ask his opinion.'

Although it seemed like a good get out for Hugo and me, I doubted whether Sinclair would thank us. Being now a super-intendent he no doubt had more than enough frustrating cases of his own to oversee without being bothered with something as nebulous as the possibly involuntary disappearance of Kyril Grimkin. I don't know exactly what Hugo told Sebastian but I was quite surprised when Hugo rang me to say we had all three been invited to lunch at the Sinclairs' house in Upminster on Sunday.

'Sebastian being as busy as always,' explained Hugo, 'he had no time for distractions from work when I first phoned him yesterday, but then he rang me back today with this invitation. I think we owe the change of heart to his wife Annabel. She'd said she'd like to meet the eccentrics who seemed to be responsible for the few real mysteries that Sebastian related to her, the rest of his work being the more common police fare of thud and blunder. Sebastian uttered the word 'eccentrics' with some relish I regret to say. Anyway, can you make it?'

I didn't much care for being lumped together with Hugo as an eccentric though I would readily concede that the word definitely applied to him. However this was an invitation not to be missed. I belatedly realised that I knew hardly anything about Sebastian Sinclair's life apart from his police work and that was no more than I gleaned from the rather few cases in which I'd become involved. Of course I knew he'd been a student of Hugo's as an anthropology undergraduate. So I was almost as interested in seeing his home as in advancing the resolution of the enigma of the Grimkins. I'd had no idea even that he lived in Upminster but as I myself was born close by in Hornchurch I had some recollection of the place though admittedly from a good few years ago.

Upminster being at the eastern end of the underground's District Line and on the main Fenchurch Street to Southend line, it made sense for me to go by train. The Sinclairs had a large house set in a reasonably sized garden in a quiet street within easy walking distance of Upminster Bridge station.

Annabel Sinclair was an attractive, friendly woman who made us very welcome. She and Sebastian had two teenage children, Steven and Lucy, who appeared for lunch and disappeared again immediately they'd eaten. When we'd finished the meal, Mrs Sinclair suggested Sebastian take us out into the garden while she loaded the dishwasher and made coffee which she'd bring out to us shortly. This sounded too good an offer to refuse or even jeopardise by making the usual ritual protests. Instead we made token contributions towards clearing the table by each taking something with us to the kitchen and then going out through the kitchen door into the garden.

The back garden had been artfully planted to screen it from neighbours and with sitting out areas sheltered on their sides but open to the sun. Sebastian cheerfully admitted his wife did most of the gardening, just employing him for some of the heavier work. He gave us a quick tour, ending in an arbour where garden chairs surrounded a low table. Annabel arrived at almost the same time with a tray loaded with all the paraphernalia for coffee. When we'd helped ourselves, Sebastian invited Hugo to say what was bothering us.

So Hugo told the tale, with Lionel and I chipping in occasionally mostly to clarify odd points where we were the ones principally involved in events. Summing up, Hugo said the facts might point to Gifford or Linda or both of them together having murdered Kyril and perhaps concealed his body in the mummy now lying in the studio.

Sebastian thought for a few minutes and then sighed.

'If this were an investigation of mine I'd reckon it was a complete shambles,' he remarked caustically. Hugo stared at him.

'That's it,' he exclaimed. 'The blue man!'

'Rave on you crazy diamond,' murmured Annabel.

'It's shine on, Mum,' interjected Lucy, who had emerged from the house and settled herself quietly among us and had appeared to be engrossed in her book and oblivious to our conversation. When it comes to multi-tasking like reading a book and eavesdropping on conversations at the same time no one is better at it than children!

'I didn't realise you were an authority on ancient rock,' smiled Annabel.

'Pink Floyd aren't really ancient,' rejoined Lucy. 'Anyway I like their sound.'

Hugo was staring at Annabel in that unfocused way that showed he was seeing only what was inside his head.

'I wonder,' he mused, 'I've been thinking in triangular terms but suppose it's a diamond.'

'Hugo, fewer riddles more answers would be welcome,' I said. He made a visible effort to reconnect with the world.

'Right. First the blue man. He's a street entertainer I suppose, a living statue. I've seen him on a few visits to York, motionless in the Shambles — that's a street in the medieval quarter of the city, formerly the street where the butchers shops were as in other towns that have streets of the same name. Now it's much more a tourist attraction with shops to match, and at times the blue man, a human figure coloured completely blue, hands and face, clothes, everything blue, and standing or sitting absolutely motion-less, occasionally deliberately moving or speaking, startling small boys and old ladies! At one time he was completely yellow I believe. I think the 'statue' of Kyril Grimkin that appeared in various streets in the City could in reality have been one of the Grimkin twins coloured totally bronze and standing absolutely motionless.

'Next the triangle. This of course is Kyril, Gifford and Kyril's wife Linda; but suppose we extend it to a diamond shape by adding in Linda's sister? What do we know about her? She's a media studies graduate and that's about all. I think it might be useful to know more about her.'

'No sweat,' said Lucy, putting her still open book face down on the grass and jumping up. She headed into the house.

Hugo and Lionel looked puzzled and I imagine I did too.

Annabel explained with a smile and a sigh.

'She'll have taken that as a challenge. She'll be up in her room on-line.'

Lucy returned ten minutes later.

'They're twins,' she said. 'Melinda and her sister who is called Belinda. They look monozygotic to me. They do their hair and make-up differently of course. They both went to Manchester Uni., Melinda did maths and then accountancy, Belinda did history of art and then media.'

'What did you actually do?' asked Sebastian.

'Was easy,' his daughter replied. 'They're both professionals so were bound to have websites. Didn't take long to sort, not so many hits with an unusual name like Bedelgart. They'd each posted a photograph of themselves on their own site. I copied and pasted the images into a fashion page that lets you see how you'd look with different hairstyles and make-up, to find out what suits you. I removed any cosmetic colouring from their portraits and gave them identical hairstyles, and they were indistinguishable.

'Under occupation, Melinda had 'Financial Director, Bedelgartwork Ltd.' I checked that out for completeness. It's a private company jointly and wholly owned by the two sisters and the Grimkin twins and its business is reported as 'Art Promotions'. It's made a loss for the last several years but I bet that's a tax dodge.'

Sebastian smiled ruefully.

'There was I thinking you only used your tablet for homework and game-playing.' Lucy made a face.

'Games are for nerds,' she said. 'I'm going indoors for a bit now.' She picked up her book and headed back to the house.

Annabel put her hand on her husband's arm.

'Now I understand why you have such difficulty fathoming the criminal mind. I can no longer keep up with what's going on in Lucy's head and I've known her all her life. What chance do you have with perfect strangers!' Sebastian chuckled.

'A lot of them aren't complete strangers: they're old lags and they certainly aren't perfect! But the main difference is most of them are our generation. I don't have a lot to do with young offenders.'

Hugo had remained silent and withdrawn through these exchanges, ever since Lucy's revelation that the sisters were twins. But now he spoke.

'I think this is giving me a headache,' he grinned rather perplexedly. 'It looks as though the Grimkin twins and the Bedelgart twins have been playing games with everyone right back to their days in Manchester. I blame the Bedelgart twins' parents! Fancy giving them names that would both shorten to Linda! Bound to give them mischievous ideas. I bet the visits Miss Farmer had when each of the Grimkin boys introduced a girlfriend called Linda were actually Kyril and Melinda and Gifford and Belinda! All straight forward except in appearances, using their shortened names to suggest things were quite different to what they were. Whether the woman we met at the studio was Melinda or Belinda I have no idea and I don't suppose you have either Lionel, do you?' Grodzinski shook his head.

Hugo reflected before continuing.

'For some reason or other my subconscious keeps throwing up the names of Gilbert and George. I believe they did pose as living statues in some of their art works but I don't feel it's just that.'

There was a short silence. A smile began to spread over Sebastian's face and then became a shout of laughter.

'Oh dear,' said Annabel, 'he's had an idea. Now he's feeling pleased with himself and rather superior to the rest of us. Any minute now he'll feel compelled to share his discovery with the rest of us.' Sebastian stopped laughing and shook his head.

'Sorry sweetheart! It is of course not you who are the cause of my mirth, nor indeed you Mr Grodzinski.' Since he didn't mention either Hugo or I, we drew our own conclusions.

'Yes,' he admitted, 'I do have an idea, I the unimaginative policeman, interested only in what the facts reveal, have an idea! It's true that all I have to go on is hearsay or, if you prefer, the expert testimony of trained scientists though not of course forensic scientists, but it does suggest something to me.'

'Come on Seb, cut the gloating and spit it out,' instructed Annabel.

'What stirred my thoughts was Hugo's mention of Gilbert and George,' he admitted. 'Why should he be reminded of them? They aren't brothers let alone twins like the Grimkins. They don't look alike despite the fact they wear identical suits whereas the Grimkins certainly do, whether dressed alike or not. So there seems to be no reason arising from the artists themselves. Of course they are all artists but that's hardly a striking resemblance in itself and their respective works of art seem quite different. Then it struck me that what Gilbert and George claim is that they are themselves works of art, that their whole lives should be regarded as art whatever it is they are doing. It makes me wonder if the Grimkins are seeking to turn the fact of their being identical twins into a facet of their artistic expression so that they can claim their lives as twins are a single work of art in itself. That would give them considerable scope for claiming tax deductible expenses,' he concluded cynically.

'I think, or at least I could believe, that the two of them realised that aspects of their lives could be thought of as a work of art and that they plan their lives to maximise that aspect, to turn their activities into one large artwork. It may be that it wasn't their own idea; perhaps the Bedelgart twins suggested and orchestrated it — the name of their company certainly seems significant. Perhaps the idea is that the creation of this 'artwork' should continue throughout their lives, being completed only by their deaths — maybe not even then! Perhaps they'll leave money to commission a joint biography as a final act.'

'It sounds more like a gigantic practical joke than art,' said Lucy who had quietly rejoined us, with her book.

'I'm sure there are many people who regard modern art as exactly that — a monstrous practical joke,' Sebastian assured his daughter.

The conversation gradually moved on to other subjects and the time passed in companionable gossip and silences in the warmth of the afternoon sun.

It seemed something of an anticlimax but there was one more act in this odd example of life's many small dramas. The events had begun to fade from my mind when I received an invitation to attend the completion of the Grimkin installation at the Grodzinski gallery in Whitechapel. Of course I went. I was intrigued by the suggestion that what I'd seen before wasn't the final work; that there was more.

If you take an interest in art it is likely you will have read about it but if not it may be that you'll have missed it. The showing got crowded out of most of the mainstream news by a story about the latest privatisation 'scamndel' but it was widely reported in the arts press and is even beginning to find a place in books covering modern movements in art.

When I arrived at the gallery I was met at the top of the stairs by Lionel who was beaming with his whole face!

'I think you'll be surprised!' was all he would say as he directed me into the space where the Grimkin exhibit was. The area where it was had been screened off with temporary curtains and the rest of the space emptied of the few free standing exhibits and filled with chairs.

I noticed that Sebastian and Annabel had been invited and also Hugo. There was an empty chair on one side of him so I occupied it. There was time to do little more than exchange greetings and for Hugo to confide that most of the other people there were from arts publications, auction houses and rival galleries — it was in effect a major publicity event, and something of a coup for the Grodzinskis.

It wasn't long before Lionel came back in and took up position in front of the curtains and conversations subsided into an expectant hush.

'Ladies and Gentlemen,' he began in his flawless English, 'some of you may already have seen this work in progress, have been able to appreciate its development at various stages, but now it is complete and on behalf of Grodzinski Galleries I am proud to be able to present it to you.' He stepped to one side and grasped a curtain cord. I just had time to wonder briefly at the absence of Gifford Grimkin from the moment of what should be his triumph before the curtains swished back and all my attention was seized by what I saw.

The installation was as before — the four plinths with their Klein bottles, their shadows, their attendant paintings and the bronze statue of Kyril Grimkin apparently gazing at the ensemble but now the shadows had been joined by four new shadows cast by four bronze nudes. Like the Kyril bronze the four new statues all had their backs to us as though staring at their shadows on the wall, each had a hand resting on their nearest plinth. The figures had all the classical poise of Greek statuary and I was reminded irresistibly of representations of the gods and goddesses of the Hellenic pantheon, as though these were perhaps the personification of each of the four dimensions in which the entities represented by the Klein bottles had their true existence.

My eyes were drawn into the exhibit to focus on the complex of shadows cast in sharp relief by the spotlighting and I now realised how integral a part of the work the lighting was. I suppose we take being able to see art for granted but the blind of course cannot; for them I suppose the plastic arts mean only sculpture although I have read of acclaimed blind painters, a phenomenon I cannot claim to understand. I resolved to ask a blind friend about this. But even as these musings flitted through my mind I was refocusing on the middle ground of the naked figures and the pottery jars on their plinths, and then to the foreground where the seemingly ever more startled bronze of Kyril leaned into the — well, the *display*. I deliberately choose to use the word display because I am uncertain whether what occurred next was an artwork in the gallery sense, an installation, a display, a happening or perhaps even a performance, or maybe more of an advertisement for the artists!

This triggered another line of thought. There is a point of view that maintains that the spectator is necessary to complete a work of art, rather as in one interpretation of quantum mechanics it is speculated that it is necessary for there to be an observer for the multifarious possibilities of reality to settle into just one. Combining the scientific and the artistic requirements, would mean that the presence of at least one person was an essential prerequisite both for the existence of the exhibit and for it being a work of art.

In some ways I was half ready for what now happened, as I assume were Hugo, Sebastian and Annabel, and I had no doubt that Lionel too knew exactly what was about to occur — it could hardly have been effected without him knowing in advance, but I imagine to almost everyone else it came as a surprise, perhaps even a shock.

The 'bronze sculpture' on the left performed a slow pirouette (a movement far from easy to effect gracefully) to finish facing the spectators, many of whom reacted with gasps of surprise. I immediately recognised it as a Grimkin twin and realised that he was flesh and blood coated in a bronze body paint. He was holding a bronze rectangle at waist height. As soon as he completed his manoeuvre he froze in as complete a stillness as before. Thus far I was half-prepared but the remainder of the performance was more unexpected.

There was a scattering of spontaneous applause and of camera flashes which seemed to act as a signal galvanising the 'statue' at the far right to pirouette in the same way revealing the other Grimkin brother, thus resolving at a stroke the question of whether he really was missing or not, whether he was alive or dead! He also held a bronze oblong.

Almost before we had time to react one of the female figures emulated them. Following Lucy's location of the Bedelgart websites I had looked at them myself and so had no difficulty recognising the face of one of them and her figure was as alluring as her countenance. Almost immediately the fourth figure turned revealing her sister. Both of them were holding bronze rectangles.

The stunned silence was this time broken by an enthusiastic and sustained round of applause. But the two sets of twins were not yet finished. Starting at the left each in turn slowly elevated their bronze oblong, at the same time rotating it forward to reveal a silver inscription on the previously hidden side. The first was inscribed 'Grimkins', the second 'Bedelgarts', the third and fourth together spelled out 'Enigma of the Image'.

The Ghoul of Gar Ghyll

'Remember my Great-Aunt Em?' asked Hugo. I had never in fact met her but Hugo had described her with considerable vividity when relating the enigma of *The Five Elderly Gentlemen* to me. He had occasionally mentioned her in other connections too, and an image of her had taken shape in my mind so I did indeed feel that in a sense I remembered her and I had formed a kind of second-hand affection for her, presumably reflecting Hugo's own feeling. She sounded a woman of good sense with a sense too of humour. So when Hugo spoke of her I listened with more attention than I sometimes afforded his monologues. I nodded.

Hugo and I had bumped into each other near Burlington House where I had been working in the library of the Royal Society of Chemistry and we had repaired to a coffee bar in Piccadilly for a natter.

'She'd not been feeling well,' he

continued, 'nothing serious, just a winter infection that had lingered on but at her age that's more worrisome than it would be for someone younger and of course it had left her a bit down in the dumps, feeling her age, which after all is considerable, and generally debilitated. The very fact that she would actually admit to not feeling well was enough to alarm me and I drove over the Pennines to see her. I suggested a holiday would do her good but she shied away from the idea as being too much bother. This further symptom of malaise strengthened my resolve. I assured her I wasn't advising her to jet off to the Caribbean or the Seychelles, just a week or two in a comfortable hotel not far from home, somewhere that she'd have her meals provided and the domestic chores all taken care of by someone else without effort or thought on her part, leaving her free to sit and read to her heart's content.

'She gradually warmed to the idea. Fortunately I had for some time been planning some research at the University of Lancaster. I decided to get Aunt Em settled and then carry out the work which would keep me within easy driving distance for a few weeks so I could keep an eye on her. I drove her the thirty or so miles from Barrow to the Theldone Hall Hotel where I felt sure she'd be well taken care of, and was pleased to hear her say it looked very nice. We enjoyed the evening meal together, plain English cooking at its best, and then I returned to the accommodation where I was staying in Lancaster.

'I looked in on her every other day to make sure all was well and that she had enough to read and was relieved to find after a few days that she was already looking better. At the end of the week I quite thought she'd insist on going home whereas I felt that another week would be sensible in order to consolidate her recovery, but to my surprise I found her quite amenable to remaining a little longer. We were having dinner in the dining room and she said she knew it was self indulgent of her but she was sure it was doing her good and besides she had grown interested in one of the other guests about whom she sensed something odd. She inclined her head towards a middle-aged woman seated on her own at a table in one of the two large windows. My aunt wouldn't say exactly what intrigued her, claiming it was rather nebulous.'

Hugo was now in full flow and I managed to restrain myself from interrupting. It seemed clear that I was to be regaled by one of his enigmas.

Hugo said his aunt had been married when quite young but tragically soon her husband had been killed in the Second World War. He'd been home on leave from the air force and with grim irony was a victim of an air raid on Barrow docks in early 1941. They'd had no children and she'd never remarried and her interest in people had been focussed on friends and acquaintances and inevitably they gradually thinned out as time passed and more and more her attention passed simply to those around her wherever she was. So Aunt Em had remained another week and Hugo popped in a couple more times to see her. On the Thursday she said it really was time she was going home although it was with some reluctance.

'I was hoping to fathom the mystery of the permanent guest,' she told Hugo, nodding at the woman she'd alluded to before, 'but I confess that far from doing so, I am more bewildered than ever.'

'Why do you call her that?' asked Hugo.

'It's Maisie's name for her. Maisie is the waitress who normally serves breakfast and she is very friendly. She says the woman's real name is Mrs. Miller, she's a widow and has been here for at least three years to Maisie's own knowledge.' She remained quietly pensive for a few minutes before continuing on a different tack. 'She's very sad.'

'Nothing unusual about that,' countered Hugo, 'there's a lot of sorrow about, so much indeed that I often wonder the human race persists. The survival instinct has to be a truly formidable driving force to overcome the sheer weight of pain, frustration, disappointment and fatigue opposing it. It seems almost a miracle that such tenacity should ever have evolved.'

'All that is irrelevant,' remarked Great-Aunt Em forthrightly — she could be devastatingly frank at times. 'It isn't that she's depressed or has given up on life. She's obsessed by something. She always sits at that same table — nothing too surprising about that, I myself have a table I prefer although if it's taken I have no problem with sitting at another. Observation suggests the same is true of other guests too.' Hugo nodded.

'It's a particular manifestation of the territorial instinct,' he remarked.

'Yes, well I'm sure that sounds very scientific,' answered Aunt Em, 'but I prefer to think of it as habit. The thing is Mrs Miller gets really upset if she doesn't get her favourite table, most particularly at breakfast; she's almost always the first person down to be sure of it. Of course she never makes a fuss if she's disappointed, she's too well-mannered for that, but I can tell, and she always finishes very quickly and then leaves abruptly. And another thing; Maisie said the other day she heard Mrs Miller talking to herself in her room, not in the way we all do at times but in a more deliberate almost instructional tone. I asked if she could make out what Mrs Miller was saying but she shook her head and said self-righteously that she was just passing, not eaves-dropping. I smiled reassuringly and nodded.

''Of course,' I said, 'I realise that. Sometimes though you just can't help but catch the odd word or phrase if it's spoken especially loudly or clearly. Of course it often doesn't make any sense which can be very frustrating.'

'Maisie frowned and said: 'Well I did hear one thing; like you said it was just a phrase, but said partikler clear like. It was,' she frowned again and wrinkled her brow and closed her eyes as though dredging up some deep buried memory. 'It was 'Go to the end of the passage and down the stairs.' Didn't seem very interesting.'

'Is it only at breakfast that she is so attached to that table?'

'I've never seen her at lunch and this is the first time since I arrived that she's been in to dinner,' answered Aunt Em, 'and Maisie says she hasn't ever seen her at lunch either but she doesn't work the dinner shift. She may be a permanent guest but she seems to be a bed and breakfast only one.'

Great-Aunt Emily observed that Mrs Miller left the hotel every morning without exception, Saturdays and Sundays included and seemed never to return before evening. As she recovered her strength — and her curiosity — Aunt Em ventured forth herself, well wrapped-up, and ascertained that the woman walked to the end of the drive and the short distance down a lane to the main road where she waited at a bus stop and caught the first service bus to come by. She asked Maisie about the buses and was told that in that direction they went to Kendal.

Sensing his aunt's frustration at being unable to fathom what she perceived to be a mystery, Hugo offered to pay for her to stay on an extra week but she wouldn't hear of doing so at his expense.

That all happened last year and this year when Hugo had visited her for a weekend and had proposed a day out Great-Aunt Emily had suggested they have a trip to Kendal and return by way of the Theldone Hall Hotel she'd stayed at and have tea there. This they did and Aunt Em was gratified to find that Maisie was still working there and even more so to find that Mrs Miller continued to be a resident and that her behaviour had never deviated in the year that had passed. As they returned to Barrow, Aunt Em told Hugo she had decided to treat herself to a summer holiday at the Theldone Hall Hotel. Hugo offered to take her there when the time came. She gratefully accepted and informed him that she had given careful thought to her proposed investigation (Hugo concealed a smile at this) and intended to begin by catching the same bus as Mrs Miller and seeing where she went.

Great-Aunt Emily duly began her investigative vacation and on her second morning at the hotel she walked down to the bus stop slightly earlier than her quarry's accustomed time. Mrs Miller seemed not to notice her at the bus stop, so absorbed was she in her own thoughts. As they boarded the bus, Aunt Emily showed the driver her pensioner's travel pass and sat near the front in case she had to get off in a hurry. In fact her fellow guest remained on the bus all the way to Kendal.

Mrs Miller got off the bus in Kendal Highgate and Great-Aunt Emily did likewise. The younger woman walked only a short distance along the street before turning into what was little more than an alleyway, called Silver How Yard. Although the buildings on either side had been converted from their original residential functions to serve as commercial premises their exteriors had been altered hardly at all, probably at the insistence of the local council and the alleyway remained too narrow for modern traffic. It sloped steeply down to its narrow end through which there was a glimpse of the sparkling surface of the River Kent. Fortunately for Aunt Em's age, Mrs Miller only went a short way down before ascending a couple of steps and disappearing through a door which she closed behind her. Aunt Emily noticed a board by the door which announced 'Dresses for Dreamers'. She stared at it, it seemed so incongruous.

Then she noticed in smaller letters below 'Customer entrance in Highgate', and it dawned on her that it must be a shop.

She returned to Highgate and looked at the shop fronts. Sure enough, the one next to the entrance to Silver How Yard was called Dresses for Dreamers. It seemed that Mrs Miller must work there in some capacity. Aunt Emily studied the shop window display which consisted of two sets of brides dresses with complementary bridesmaids dresses and page outfits. It was clearly a wedding outfitters. She couldn't imagine many boys would allow themselves to be coerced into one of those suits though! It was all a far cry from her own day she thought. Making up her mind, she pushed open the shop door and entered to an accompanying peal of wedding bells.

The shop was brightly lit and two dresses in dazzling white made it seem even more so. There were dresses in other colours too which struck Aunt Em as strange when she thought back to her own youth but she reflected it was probably just as much a matter of changing taste as an increasing acceptance of realities. There were also small gifts for sale suitable for people not closely connected to the couple getting married but wishing to give something. There was a middle-aged woman standing behind the counter and she smiled at Great-Aunt Emily.

'Hullo,' said the latter, and smiled back. 'I'm not getting married myself.' The woman laughed.

'You might be surprised at how many people do so in their later years. Not so many of them go for the full works though.'

'That's a tactful way of referring to my age.' Aunt Em realised she hadn't given enough thought to what she was going to say but she was saved from an embarrassing silence by a sudden shaft of inspired deceit which when she recollected it later made her feel both ashamed at the ease of her duplicity and at the same time guiltily pleased at her facility.

'In fact I must admit that I'm not looking to buy anything at all. It's just that I've a great-niece — well she's the grand-daughter of an old friend really,' she embroidered with increasingly shameless mendacity, 'who's getting married in America. My friend has written to me about it, saying how different it all is to when we were girls and I thought I'd just come and see what dresses are like these days.' The woman nodded.

'I understand,' she replied and Aunt Em hoped she didn't really! 'Do have a look round. The two dresses in the window are quite traditional so that people can see immediately that this is a bridal shop. Most of the dresses we sell we make up from design books in whatever colour and material people want.'

'I suppose that's quite unusual; I mean it seems most clothes these days are simply bought off the peg, even for very special occasions.' Aunt Em reflected that she'd never bought any clothes that weren't ready made and then, rather sadly, that there'd only been one really special occasion in her life, when she herself got married and then she'd made her own dress. Unless, she thought, she counted funerals as special and they now came along with such frequency that there was no question of buying a new outfit to wear although she tried to dress respectfully for them. People seemed nowadays to go to them in almost anything. She realised the woman was regarding her sympathetically. She'll be thinking I'm an ounce short of a pound she admonished herself.

'I mean, having anything made to measure must be so expensive with wages being what they are.'

'Oh it isn't just the wages, it's finding anyone with the skill and patience to do proper dress-making,' answered the woman frankly. 'I don't think they teach it to girls in school anymore. But I'm very lucky. Mrs Miller who helps me in the shop is a perfect treasure, not only knows what she's doing but is skilful and patient too. And she's a worker, unlike some! Chits of girls call themselves dress-designers these days instead of plain dress-maker and well they might since their idea of making a dress seems to be fastening bits of material together with tacking stitches instead of neat and proper stitching that will last.'

Great-Aunt Emily made a show of

looking more closely at things while she thought furiously of what else she could ask.

'I suppose she's been with you a long time,' she improvised desperately and rather inanely.

'It feels as though she's always been here,' reflected the shop keeper, 'but I think that's because since she started she's been so reliable. In fact it can't be much more than about three or four years since she suddenly turned up looking for work. I admit I was a bit sceptical at first. The vagaries of the retail trade have made me very cynical I'm afraid but there was something, well, stolid about her and I was desperate for someone. I've never regretted taking her on. Of course she isn't perfect, who is? But she's only got one slight drawback as far as I am concerned.'

The shopkeeper paused for breath. Aunt Em felt slightly uneasy listening to all these confidences about a woman only yards away but having set the shop woman going it didn't look as though it would be easy to bring her to a halt; and besides she still hoped to hear something which would clear up the mystery and in the meantime she felt she was coming to understand a side of Mrs Miller of which Maisie clearly had no knowledge. She suppressed her discomfort and stared encouragingly at her informant.

'Perhaps I shouldn't be gossiping like this but she is just a bit mysterious and I am curious, it's human nature after all. Well she seems happy to work all day and every day, work late too if we're under pressure but I insist she has at least one day a week off and hers is usually Thursday but every now and again, perhaps once a month, she takes Wednesday instead and I never know until the day. I'll get a hasty sounding telephone call on the morning about an hour before she usually arrives, to tell me. That's all and since she is rarely needed to serve in the shop — indeed that would be a waste of her needlework skill — that it's a negligible inconvenience, I'm certainly not complaining.'

Aunt Em felt a brief surge of satisfaction. Her instinct told her that this was the clue for which she'd been fishing. She didn't yet see what its significance might be, but it was an oddity to add to the other curiosities she'd accumulated. Her earlier qualms had now subsided and she was beginning to enjoy herself again and the other woman seemed equally content to prattle on while Aunt Em would listen. However nothing else was said to alert her detective antennae and a little while later another customer entered and Aunt Em took the opportunity to say farewell and how much she'd enjoyed their talk.

Her investigation had stimulated Aunt Em's appetite and she had a good plain lunch in an old-fashioned department store, did a bit of shopping for impulse buys which, she told herself were quite all right to make if she did them quickly and then bolstered this highly dubious logic by reasoning that if she happened to meet Mrs Miller on the bus back it would appear that she'd just made the trip into Kendal to shop. Feeling tired with so much walking the ups and downs of the ancient town's streets and alleyways, she stopped not far from the bus station and ordered afternoon tea which included a scone with jam and butter and cream, a treat she ought to indulge in more often she told herself — in obedience to the notion that a little of what you fancy does you good.

In the bus on the way back to the hotel, Great-Aunt Emily stared out at the hedgerows and fields bordering the road and across them to woodlands and to the hills beyond but without really seeing the lush countryside. She was pondering the one really interesting thing she'd learned. Mrs Miller took just one day off a week, usually a Thursday but sometimes a Wednesday. Remembering Hugo's reasoning in the enigma of *The Five Elderly Gentlemen*, she felt sure it was what Mrs Miller did on the one day a week she wasn't at work that was the key to the puzzle and she felt instinctively that it was the occasional Wednesdays that were significant.

Then it occurred to her that she had learned something else that might be relevant. Mrs Miller had started work at the bridal shop at about the same time as she'd taken up residence at the Theldone Hall Hotel. It was very odd too that she worked so hard presumably so that she could remain at the hotel rather than seek somewhere cheaper to live, somewhere closer to Kendal too. Aunt Em could not herself have afforded to reside at the Theldone Hall Hotel permanently — she'd used some savings to make her extended stay possible as it was and making some reasonable estimates about costs and wages she decided Mrs Miller had to have some income at least from another source. She must have a compelling reason to be clinging to that hotel despite the difficulties. She was sure it couldn't be just the pleasure of the illusion of gracious living it offered. It seemed to Aunt Em it was most likely to be because of its location.

Abruptly these two fragments of the puzzle were joined together by a third clue — the other woman's obsession with the table in the window. How obtuse she was being she chided herself. In fact it was obvious. That window had a distant view of the road, the road to Kendal. Of course the road went both ways and in the other direction it led ultimately to Barrow. Mrs Miller must be watching out for something going either to or from one of those places or somewhere on the road to them. The shipyard came immediately to mind when she thought of Barrow, the yard where Britain's nuclear submarines were built. Could her fellow guest at the hotel be some sort of spy? Or perhaps she was the spotter for a gang of thieves, alerting them to particular lorries travelling the road! Aunt Em reined in her imagination sharply; she was being too fanciful. No, all her instincts about people told her that Mrs Miller's preoccupation was something far more personal.

Eventually she reached the inevitable conclusion that she needed more information and came back to her first thoughts: she needed to know where Mrs Miller went on the days she wasn't at the shop. Well, tomorrow was Wednesday so she might be able to find out then.

The next morning Great-Aunt Emily was down to breakfast a little earlier than usual to be sure not to miss whatever might happen but was not surprised to find that Mrs Miller was already in her customary place and seemed as ever not to notice Aunt Em or anyone else. She looked especially alert throughout breakfast, her attention riveted on the distant road as she mechanically ate her usual cereal, grapefruit, and toast and marmalade and drank two cups of tea. Eventually however, she sighed, folded her napkin and left the dining room.

Great-Aunt Emily followed her down to the bus stop on the main road. When she reached it she gave her quarry a friendly nod and received a wan smile in return. Aunt Em judged it would be profitless to attempt conversation then, the woman was so obviously preoccupied.

That day followed the pattern of the previous one and Aunt Emily learned nothing new but consoled herself with the thought that tomorrow could be the significant one.

On Thursday, in the middle of breakfast, Mrs Miller suddenly stiffened and shortly afterwards left the dining room and went upstairs, taking Aunt Em by surprise although she had thought she was ready for it. She reluctantly abandoned her slice of toast with butter and marmalade half-eaten and hastened to her own room where she got ready as quickly as she could and went back downstairs just in time to see Mrs Miller hurry out through the front entrance. Although Aunt Em walked as fast as she was able the younger woman had the advantage of her and soon disappeared round a bend in the drive where it curved away between thick shrubs. When Aunt Em reached the gates on to the road and looked towards the bus stop the other woman was nowhere to be seen.

Great-Aunt Emily castigated herself for having lost an opportunity through her own tardiness, an opportunity that was unlikely to occur again until the next week. Then she saw the bus coming and realised she wasn't actually late; so where could the woman have gone? Aunt Emily stood well back from the kerb and let the bus go by, following it with her eyes — and there she was! The stop for buses in the other direction was about a hundred yards back along the road, where there was a shelter and Mrs Miller had just emerged from it, presumably in readiness for the imminent arrival of the service in that direction. Aunt Em crossed the busy carriageways, at some risk to her safety, and walked confidently along to the stop. She pantomimed surprise at again encountering her fellow guest, but her performance was lost on the other whose attention was all focussed inward.

No one else had boarded the bus with them but there were already some passengers aboard and Aunt Emily felt well camouflaged by their presence. It seemed strange to be heading in the direction of Barrow. Was her investigation taking her back to her home town? But the bus did not stay on the Barrow road. After a mile or so it turned sharply left into a narrow lane between hedges. It crossed the River Kent and began to wind upwards onto the higher ground towards Silverdale. Aunt Em was soon confused by the twisty route which seemed designed to visit every hamlet in the district. It was all a bit mesmerising and she was taken by surprise when at a stop which seemed in the middle of nowhere much, Mrs Miller quickly rose and alighted. Before Aunt Em could react the bus was off again. She just caught sight of a gap in the hedge set with two massive gate posts on one of which was a sign headed Cruikscar Castle. With a sigh of exasperation, Great-Aunt Emily settled back in her seat. She'd have to go on to the next stop and then catch a bus back, trusting that her quarry had gone to the castle.

She was out of luck. The bus seemed to have completed its tour of villages and there were no more stops until it reached Arnside where she got off and the bus resumed its journey to Carnforth and Lancaster. She then discovered to her dismay that the return service was not until the late afternoon. Aunt Em made the best of things and walked along the estuary front. She enjoyed lunch and afternoon tea in a pleasant cafe and browsed in such shops as there were including an art gallery which she felt Hugo might have appreciated more than she did, before catching the bus back to the hotel. She had decided that she would visit Cruikscar Castle the following day to try and decide what might have drawn Mrs Miller to it.

In accordance with her plan, the next day Aunt Em got off the bus at the gate of Cruikscar Castle and walked up a drive lined with trees. Rounding a bend she saw the castle in front of her. Calling it a castle was no grandiose boast. It clearly had begun as a real fortress not just a folly of would-be country gentry. There were no pillars, no portico. Four massive towers stood at its corners and between them stretched solid walls built by a wary castellan, ready for defence against marauding armies from whatever direction but most especially from the north should invading Scots reach as far south as Westmorland.

Massive oaken doors stood open to permit passage through the front wall to the courtyard in the centre of which stood a central keep. There were three easily negotiated steps up to a massive oaken door which opened into a gloomy hall lined with suits of battered armour.

The walls above were decorated with swords, daggers, pikes, crossbows and muskets; tattered flags and banners hung from high ceiling beams. On the right side was a highly polished table of dark wood covered with guide books, postcards, leaflets and all the usual money garnering rubbish of a funds hungry country estate. An attendant seated behind it uttered a no-nonsense 'Two pounds for Seniors' and held out what looked like a raffle ticket in return.

'Would you like a guide book?' she asked. Somewhat reluctantly Aunt Em decided it might be relevant to her curiosity about Mrs Miller's visit so she rather grudgingly stumped up. Having completed the transaction, the woman then handed her a cassette player equipped with earphones.

'And the loan of this is included in the cost of your ticket. It's to be returned as you leave.'

'Hm, you might have mentioned that before selling me the book!' commented Great-Aunt Emily.

'You may not appreciate it, but this is an important and historic building, the home of a distinguished family,' the woman announced haughtily. Aunt Em treated her to a stony stare and moved on without comment. She followed the directions on the audio guide with a feeling that they had some significance other than the obvious. She admitted to herself that the castle did indeed contain much of interest. It was as she was following one of the verbal directions to 'Go to the end of the passage' that she realised what the guide reminded her of — it was the fragment overheard by Maisie from outside Mrs Miller's room. Had the latter been listening to one of these guides? But then Maisie said it was Mrs Miller's voice she heard. The audio guide Aunt Em was listening to was a man's voice. Aunt Em added the conundrum to the others she had accumulated in her mind.

Having completed the tour of the house, Aunt Em strolled round the gardens and glasshouses. She didn't try and see them all but was grateful when she found a seat in one of the greenhouses among a display of unremarkable but pretty geraniums. There was a cafeteria in one of the castle's outhouses where she consumed a snack midday. She made sure she was at the castle gate in good time to catch the return bus service as she had no wish to be stranded there. As the bus trundled along the lanes she reviewed her day. There was nothing about what she had seen that seemed likely to be the cause of the particular interest she sensed Mrs Miller had in the place.

That evening thinking over what she had learned so far, Aunt Em decided that field work (she liked the sound of that even though it was one of Hugo's phrases!) had taken her as far as it could. She would have to talk to Mrs Miller if she wanted to know more, and she did even though she felt slightly guilty about her curiosity.

By the next morning she was feeling less inclined to barge in on whatever was worrying the other woman but when she went down to breakfast, fate gave her a gentle push. A large party had arrived at the hotel the previous night and they were all down early so that the dining room was much more crowded than usual. It was obvious that Aunt Em would have to share a table with someone and it seemed the natural thing to do to join Mrs Miller. After all they were both regulars in a sense.

'Do you mind if I join you?' she asked. 'It's unusually crowded this morning.'

'No, of course not.' Great-Aunt Em sat down and ordered her usual breakfast.

'I'm not sure what to do today; the weather looks a bit unsettled. I might go into Kendal again,' she ventured.

'It's a pleasant town,' responded Mrs Miller. 'There's quite a lot to see even when it's wet.' Aunt Em nodded.

'I was here in the hotel last year,' said Aunt Em. 'I'm sure I saw you here then too.' She was pleased to find that the other was not at all aloof. It's true she kept her eyes on the distant road all the time with only occasional glances at Aunt Em, but she managed to do so without being distracted. Indeed it seemed after a while that she was glad to talk. Eventually she showed signs of going.

'I work in Kendal,' she said, 'and it's time I was leaving. Perhaps I'll see you on the bus if you do decide to go in today.'

Of course Aunt Em seized the opportunity to further their acquaintance and made sure she was down at the bus stop in time to catch the bus Mrs Miller travelled on and contrived also to be on the same bus back in the evening, by which time they were on first name terms. When she reviewed what she had learned that day she was well pleased. Next morning although there were plenty of empty tables at breakfast it seemed natural that they should again share a table and they soon took up their exchange of confidences where it had lapsed the previous day.

'Jim used to work in the shipyard,' said Edna Miller, 'until he was made redundant. Although he was a skilled craftsman his skills were not in demand after the government of the day decided to give up defending the country so it could afford policies it hoped would bribe the electorate into voting it back into power. Jim wasn't one of those aristocrats of labour too proud to take a job that might be deemed beneath him if it meant it could provide us with a living. Of course it was inevitable that his bring-home pay diminished but I got part-time work to fill the gap even though he felt bad about that. He did a variety of jobs, none of which lasted long; too often his employers were ruined by the rapacity of their bankers and their demands for ever greater security and returns for the money they deigned to lend struggling businesses.'

Mrs Miller was evidently a well-read and articulate woman with strong views on what was wrong with the times.

'Anyway, one of the jobs he got to help us pay the mortgage was at Cruikscar Castle as a general handyman, fixing anything about the place that needed fixing. There was a lot of it and he worked as hard as he always did but he didn't complain about that. They got a very good return on the miserable amount they paid him.

'Still, he was content enough at first — he wasn't one for railing against his lot in life, but as time went by I could see something began to irk him. It wasn't just that the Dowager Lady Cruikscar and her son the present Lord Cruikscar were so distant and stuck-up. Despite their arrogance they were short of money and to make ends meet the Castle had for many years been opened to visitors as so many are. Jim felt visitors were poorly rewarded for the money they handed over for the privilege of shuffling around the decaying pile. He reckoned with very little additional effort and a modicum of goodwill the family could provide a much better experience and almost certainly boost their visitor numbers and hence profits as a result.'

But then her husband had vanished. He went out to work as usual one morning but didn't return in the evening. Mrs Miller began to get anxious when he hadn't appeared more than an hour after his usual time and she phoned the Castle but it was a recorded message announcing that office hours were nine to five and that full information for visitors was available on the Cruikscar website. By ten in the evening she was convinced something serious had happened, she was sure he would otherwise have contacted her somehow. She telephoned the police.

The officer she spoke to did his best to reassure her but said that he would phone around the local hospital accident and emergency departments. When he phoned her back he had no news for her and endeavoured to convince her that no news was good news. She was not persuaded but could think of nothing else to do.

The next day she phoned Cruikscar Castle again but no one she spoke to could tell her anything. It was assumed her husband had left there when he finished work yesterday as usual and it was certain that he had not turned up today. Mrs Miller went herself to the police station. She spoke to a uniformed sergeant and they once more phoned round the hospitals but no one of her husband's description had been admitted. It was explained to her that very many people went missing temporarily and soon turned up and that it was official policy to wait a few days before making enquiries except in the case of a minor.

However he agreed that her husband didn't seem to be the sort of man who would behave as some did and said he'd make some unofficial enquiries.

Nothing came of these nor of more intensive investigations thereafter. Jim Miller seemed indeed to have vanished into thin air and with nothing to go on the police gradually wound down their efforts. Edna was not about to give up however.

'I was convinced that the answer had something to do with that cursed castle,' she said firmly. 'I went there several times and talked to everyone I could, including Lady Cruikscar. Most were sympathetic but she was not; downright rude best describes her attitude. She finally told me to stop being an interfering busy-body otherwise she'd have a word with the local police superintendent. Her reaction was totally out of proportion. The trouble was, they are too penny-pinching to employ enough staff and she regularly mans the reception desk herself so I was effectively frustrated in my efforts to find out anything.

'Of course as he wasn't turning up to

work Jim's wages were stopped and what little I earned fell short of what I needed to keep up our mortgage payments. In the end I had little option but to sell the house. We had cleared some of the outstanding purchase cost so it gave me a bit of capital. I decided to use it to allow me to keep searching for Jim. The staff I'd talked to before I was warned off by Lady High-and-Mighty all seemed to have a liking for Jim — he was always easy to get along with and he never made any fuss. He just got on with his work and people appreciated him. So they were happy to talk to me, not only about that last day he'd been at work but just generally

'After I was shown the door, as I was leaving I told one of them I'd been forbidden to return and she confided that Lady Cruikscar was in the habit of going to Kendal once a week to be pampered — hair done and such like — and that Bert the chauffeur always drove her there in her Rolls Royce Wraith. She said whatever her ladyship might decree, they'd be pleased to see me if I wanted to come when she was away.

'The first time I went to the Castle I'd caught the bus from Barrow into Kendal and then caught the Lancaster round-about route from there. After that I realised that I could get off the bus from Barrow and wait for the Lancaster service here. I'd noticed this hotel on one of the visits I'd made and realised that the Castle car would have to pass it taking Lady Cruikscar to Kendal. I came here one afternoon for tea and found that from the dining room windows it was possible to see all the traffic using the road. When our house was sold and I had to move out, I put our furniture in store and took a room here. After a few weeks I'd worked out that she seemed always to go to Kendal on a Wednesday or Thursday and that she went quite early, while breakfast was still being served in the hotel in fact. To eke out the bit of money I had I got a job in Kendal where I go except on the days I spot the Castle Rolls.

'Ever since I've been poking about at the Castle as often as I can go there looking for some clue as to Jim's fate. I do have something to go on.

'This was among his work things,' she said, taking a booklet from her bag. 'Judging by the old-fashioned monochrome photo on the cover and even more by the price of three shillings and sixpence it's a very old guide to the castle. Jim pencilled notes here and there in the margins. I can remember him reading and re-reading it sometimes of an evening with a puzzled expression on his face. He said he'd come across it in the tool shed he used at the castle. I asked him what he found so intriguing and he said it seemed odd that some of the interesting things that used to be on display no longer were. You'd think, he'd said, that as the stately homes market has got more competitive there'd be an effort to show more rather than less. I can't help thinking that his curiosity about it may have had something to do with his disappearance. I've been following up his notes as best I could whenever the dragon is away from her lair.'

She leaned forward confidingly.

'Jim had salvaged an audio guide that was being discarded for some reason and he'd shown me how to use it. I found I could edit it with the help of our own cassette player and insert directions to places in the old guide that were not included in the new audio tour. I felt that if I was asked about where I was going I could claim that I was just following the audio instructions.' That, thought Aunt Em, accounted for the snatch of speech Maisie had overheard.

'The trouble is some of the places are locked and they are probably the important ones. I don't know if Jim got into them and if so how he did it.' She sighed. 'I'm afraid I'm just not going to be able to go on much longer. I can't stay here indefinitely, the little bit of capital I had is draining away.

'However, I'm looking forward to next week,' Mrs Miller went on in a more optimistic tone, 'because my niece Petronella is joining me for a few days. She's going to help me try to puzzle out what's happened to Jim. I call her my niece but I can't remember exactly what sort of relation she is, some sort of cousin twice removed I think. She's the daughter of a third or fourth cousin who lived quite close by when we were all younger. She and her husband moved to Wearside where he got a job when times were lean in the Barrow shipyard and they never came back. Of course that was a long time ago; there's no ship building in Sunderland now. It's awful how things have changed. Anyway, their daughter Petronella was the same age as our own daughter Julie and she used to come and stay with us for a fortnight in the summer holidays and our Julie would go to Sunderland for a fortnight. The pair of them got on very well together.' She burrowed into her handbag again and brought out a small leather wallet, opening it to reveal two photographs. 'That's our Julie — she and her husband live in Australia now — and this is Petronella.'

Great-Aunt Emily studied the photos with interest, particularly the one of Petronella.

'They're both bonny girls,' she said thoughtfully. 'I've been thinking. There maybe someone else who could help with your problem. My great-nephew Hugo is an anthropologist — he gets paid to study how people live and behave — at least I think that's what he does. He's a professor or some such at a university. But in his spare time — of which he seems to have an awful lot — he's quite good at solving mysteries. I think this is just the sort of thing that would interest him. He keeps saying he needs a holiday. I could suggest he comes and spends a few days with me. After all it was he who persuaded me to stay here in the first place, when I'd been under the weather. He thought it would do me good and for once he was right. He has a friend who sometimes helps him. Perhaps he'd come too. Between us we ought to be able to sort it out.'

At this point Hugo's narrative came to an abrupt end.

'So how are you fixed?' he asked. 'Could you use a few days relaxation from your doubtless fascinating researches? The Theldone Hall Hotel isn't as expensive as it otherwise might be, possibly because it isn't smartly modern, more a picture of decayed elegance, but probably the more comfortable as a result. For some reason

Aunt Em is very insistent that she thinks you could be a real help.'

Truth to tell, my present investigation was stuck. The results from the latest experiments were inconsistent with the previous ones and I couldn't figure out why. It's true that chemistry has as much in common with the art of cookery as with the science of atoms and molecules and sometimes it simply doesn't turn out well but I wasn't happy just to accept that. I needed to devise some new experiments to get to the bottom of the contradictory results. So on impulse I said yes and thus it was that a few days later I was at the Theldone Hall Hotel.

My room was very large, about four times the size of a typical room in a modern custom built hotel and so had space for comfortable furniture instead of the pretence of such usually provided in more recent establishments. It also had two large windows with views across an extensive lawn towards a main road on which I could see diminutive vehicles speeding in both directions in a demonstration of apparent futility. Adjacent to this room was a generously proportioned bathroom with bath, shower and all the usual appurtenances.

I unpacked my bag, managing to fill only two drawers of the dozen available and to occupy about a foot of the five foot hanging rail in the wardrobe. I took a deep breath and although this left sufficient air in the luxurious volume of the room to keep me alive for several days, I raised one of the sash windows a few inches, not without difficulty, and savoured the warm fresh air and the hum of distant traffic this admitted.

I descended the broad staircase — wide enough for two or three lanes of guests to travel in opposite directions at the same time — from the gallery landing to the entrance hall which was in keeping with the grand scale of the rest of the building, thinking Theldone Hall must have been quite a grand house in its former existence and briefly enjoying the feeling of being grand myself. I went into the bar which had been fashioned by walling off the end of the hall that had once extended the full depth of the building from the impressive front entrance to the magnificent fenestration looking out into the gardens behind the hotel. The bar itself was in consequence less imposing than the rest but comfortable enough and more suited to ordinary scale people like me!

Hugo was already there, sitting on a chintz sofa and chatting to an elderly comfortably proportioned woman who could only be his great-aunt. She regarded me steadily for a disconcerting minute or so and then gave a half nod as though making up her mind that I was about as expected.

'I'm very pleased to meet you at last,' she said, 'although I feel I know you quite well already having read your stories which are much more interesting than Hugo's.' I looked quizzically at him.

'Aunt Em means my scientific papers,' he said. I grinned.

'Thank you,' I said to Great-Aunt Emily, 'I'm pleased you liked them.'

We exchanged the ritual remarks about the weather that the relaxed atmosphere suggested would be appropriate before

Aunt Em alluded to the reason for our presence there.

'I've invited Edna Miller and her niece Petronella Bennet to join us for dinner,' she said. 'I know how busy you are and we don't want to waste any time. We could discuss strategy and be ready to start your investigation straight after breakfast tomorrow.' I hoped Hugo had some ideas because I didn't. However all my doubts were blown away when I saw Petronella. I can't really describe what I felt at that moment and indeed there is no reason for me to do so. I'll simply say that I was overwhelmed by the sight of her and every minute of her acquaintance reinforced my initial thankfulness that I had joined Hugo in this probably doomed undertaking and my awareness of what I would have missed had I not come as I so easily might not have done. Such is the nature of chance, a wholly different matter in human terms to its mathematical significance.

As the five of us sat with our coffee at the end of the meal, Mrs Miller showed us her husband's copy of the old guide.

Hugo studied Jim Miller's notes carefully. (I'm afraid I was rather distracted). When he had finished he asked Edna Miller if she had anything to add to what she'd told Great-Aunt Emily previously. She hadn't but her niece had.

'Before I came I did a background search of the Cruikscar family on the net,' said Petronella. 'It dredged up a lot of stuff they don't allude to in any edition of their guidebooks. The original Earls of Cruikscar were Norman thugs who were granted their estates as a reward for their part in the 'pacifying' of the north after the Norman Conquest — nowadays their behaviour would be classed as genocide. The family name of the present incumbents however was originally Bramble. The family made its money in the slave trade, operating out of Liverpool, sailing to West Africa loaded with trinkets which they exchanged for slaves whom they transported for sale across the Atlantic, mainly to the West Indies, returning to England with cargoes of cotton from the plantations. By the time the slave trade was outlawed within the British Empire in 1807 they had themselves acquired a number of plantations in the new world where they grew cotton and tobacco using slave labour.

'When slavery itself was at last made illegal throughout the Empire in 1833 they profited from the compensation paid to slave owners for the emancipation of the slaves although they continued to exploit them as a cheap labour force wherever they could. With all the money they'd accumulated they bought Cruikscar Castle from its impoverished aristocratic owner, the then head of the Bramble family marrying the former owner's only daughter, taking their name and setting themselves up as seigneurs. They bought a barony by contributing funding to the governing party of the day and adopted the style Baron Cruikscar of Cruikscar. A not uncommon pattern among the nobility of England I fancy.'

'From what my aunt has told me,' said Hugo to Edna Miller, 'you've looked into most of the things that puzzled your husband, like the disappearance of wax figures representing servants who would once have worked at the castle from the rooms where they would have performed their duties, and the collections of stuffed animals and birds, and of butterflies but you haven't found any sign of them either although you've looked in many of the places that are also no longer on public view like the kitchens and larders and pantries. You found the art gallery which is now closed to visitors and noticed that a number of paintings were missing. They of course might have been sold and the diminution of the collection might be the reason it's no longer open. The main places you haven't looked in are the stables and the ice house, and both of those you found locked just as your husband noted. There was a pencilled note in the guide he left with you about the keys on the bunch he had from the castle to the effect that two of them seemed to be no use to him in his work. It may be that they fitted the locked buildings. I take it you don't have his work keys?'

Mrs Miller shook her head. 'He had them with him that last day.'

'Well it would seem sensible to make an

effort to gain access to the stables and the ice house before considering any other approaches we might make. Tomorrow is Wednesday so we must hope Lady Cruikscar goes to Kendal and gives us all an opportunity to visit the Castle. If she doesn't, the rest of us will go without you so as not to make it obvious that we are other than casual visitors.'

Luck was with us and Mrs Miller spotted the Wraith while we were all having breakfast together. We wasted no time in getting ready and soon the five of us were in Hugo's Range Rover heading along the lanes to Cruikscar Castle. On arrival we parked, paid the entrance fee, and set out to explore the grounds. I say explore but Edna Miller knew her way around them already and we quickly reached our first objective.

The stable block was at a little distance from the castle itself but the approach to it was well-screened and we met nobody on our way there. It was an imposing edifice built in the late nineteenth century by the third baron who was obsessed with horse racing. There was an arched gateway leading into a spacious courtyard with stables on all four sides. Hugo led the way to double doors on the left sides. They were secured with a large padlock but after the successful resolution of an earlier enigma (that of *The Expensive Daub*) Hugo had prevailed upon its main perpetrator to share some expertise he'd acquired earlier in his career in a different field of malefaction — that of lock-picking. Hugo soon had the lock open.

The interior was spacious, one might almost say it was luxuriously proportioned for a stable. Against the back wall were a number of large stalls, each one separated from its neighbour by a substantial dividing wall. The fronts were open to the wide cobbled corridor that ran next to the front wall of the building. These stalls which once had accommodated horses had been refurbished as nineteenth century shop units. The first of these was evidently a bakers, complete with counter, scales and cash register, trays of imitation loaves of various kinds and glass cases with luridly coloured and fantastically shaped counterfeit cakes. A wax figure of a shopkeeper stood behind the counter with its hands resting on it. Old metal advertising plates adorned the walls.

The next one along represented a butchers with plastic joints, fowls, cutlets and so on arrayed in enamel trays. Then came a greengrocers, an ironmongers, a pharmacy — which I found especially interesting — and a bookshop, the latter seemingly not a great deal different from a present day one.

The displays were interesting and it was difficult to see any reason for them no longer being open to the public. It's true that Hugo had a reservation about the toy shop, pointing out a glass cabinet holding a collection of erotic dolls, but that could easily have been removed if thought unsuitable in a shop purveying things for children, which it probably was. We also had some reservations about the final shop in this indoor 'street'.

It was an undertakers with several coffins stacked against its wall and costumes and necessities for a typical Victorian funeral and for its preliminaries displayed in cases and half-opened drawers. This stable unit had been a double one so that the undertaker's 'shop' had an inner room glimpsed through a half open door which revealed a table for preparing the corpse for viewing by mourners and a further display of instruments of the trade. All in all it was an unsettling exhibition.

After the undertaker's parlour there was a solid looking floor to ceiling wall with a narrow staircase beside it. As we prepared to ascend, Hugo murmured to me:

'You might have a look in those coffins, just in case, and a quick glance at that inner room.' I gave him an unfriendly look, but saw the sense in his suggestion — just not why it should be me who did it. Still I complied. Fortunately the lids were not fastened down, the wood was only pine and with a bit of heaving and shoving I could get a peek in the bottom two as well as the top one. They were all empty and the inner room afforded no obvious hiding place for a body. I hastened to climb after the others and found them in a long well-lit loft.

On the walls hung a collection which it

quickly became obvious was entirely made up of mildly erotic art. The canvases looked as though they were all by nineteenth century artists, minor masters such as the Yorkshireman William Etty, and a variety of French painters including Bouguereau and Gerome. Hugo pointed to one by the latter. It depicted a naked woman surrounded by men in Arab dress.

'*The Slave Market*,' he said. 'I am sure that is a copy. The original is in the Sterling and Francine Clark Art Institute in Massachusetts I believe. It's not the sort of reminder of an infamous family history any decent man would want to hang on his wall but I imagine it and the other paintings were in the collection which was once on display but is no longer, although these drawings are unlikely to have been in any serious collection.' With a gesture he indicated a number of pencil sketches of women in minimalist attire also arrayed along the wall. They looked modern and seemed to have no significant artistic merit unlike the paintings which were well crafted in the academician style.

'It's very suggestive in more than the obvious sense,' he went on.

We returned to the head of the stair next to which was a door. He opened it and led us through into another loft at a right-angle to the first, evidently above the rear side of the square. This one was full of what might loosely be described as stuffed animals. There were hundreds of them, native to many parts of the world, many in glass cases but some free standing. They were well lit by skylights.

'This is a very creditable collection of taxidermy,' said Hugo. 'Why on earth is it hidden away?' About half way along he stopped and examined a cat which although on a pedestal was not enclosed.

'This is I think different. It looks to me as though it has been mummified rather than skinned and stuffed. The Egyptians of course mummified animals in considerable numbers and cats were favoured subjects but it has not generally been the practise in modern times. Whether this is an ancient mummy or a more recent one I am not expert enough to tell.' There were other mummified exhibits in the collection, some of them appearing to be rather badly done. We didn't spend too long examining the display but pressed on to the loft's far end and turned the corner into the third side, there being no dividing wall at this angle. There proved nothing of interest in that loft nor in the one on the final side which continued uninterrupted over the gateway to the courtyard. There was no access back to the first side we'd explored so we retraced our steps and descended the stair up which we'd come.

'Did you say there was a door in the far side of the inner parlour of the undertaker's?' asked Hugo. I nodded.

'Perhaps we'll find the missing figures that used to be displayed in the rooms through there,' he said. We followed his lead, rather reluctantly on my part as I was beginning to feel that we were wasting our time. I had of course already seen the inner room, with its solid table used, presumably, to lay out bodies for washing, embalming and dressing in their coffin clothes. We didn't linger there but passed quickly through to the room beyond and found ourselves in the lower floor of the area below the collection of stuffed animals. It seemed to be used for nothing more than rather untidy storage of lumber although in the second stall there were some interesting looking clear glass carboys, full or half-full of colourless liquid. I eased the bung out of one and sniffed it warily. I recognised the smell instantly.

'Formalin,' I said, 'as surely as I can tell without running a spectrum. It may be that some of the specimens above were preserved in the not too distant past. The process might well have been carried out in the undertaker's parlour, given the proximity of these materials to it.'

We decided we'd seen everything there was to see and so we left the stable block after Hugo had expertly refastened the padlock.

'That explains some of the things that had puzzled Jim Miller. I wonder if he managed to get in there too,' said Hugo.

'He didn't say anything to suggest he had,' answered Edna Miller, 'But he was very pensive at times.'

'I've seen nothing yet that would account for her husband's disappearance,' remarked Hugo in an aside to me. I agreed.

The ice house was in a more remote part of the grounds. It was used in bygone times to store ice and packed snow collected in the depths of winter so that food could be chilled for preservation in summer months. These stores were usually in a deep cellar or some such to take advantage of the insulating properties of stone. At Cruikscar it seemed a natural cave had been adapted for the purpose. It was situated in a narrow ravine called Gar Ghyll, a rock-strewn bracken clothed gulley. Mrs Miller led us through the gardens and into a small wood at the further side of which was the ghyll and a short distance in, rough stone work had been erected to seal off the entrance to a cave in the side of the cleft. There was a wooden door set in the masonry and secured with a stout looking padlock. Once again Hugo's nefarious skills were utilised to spring the lock and we found ourselves looking into a gloomy opening at the top of a flight of steps.

Leaving the door open behind us to provide some light we descended the stone stair into a gloom otherwise illuminated only by the torch thoughtfully brought by Hugo who naturally was in the lead. After the steps turned two right angles the torch was all the light we had so Hugo kept it directed down at the steps, to guide our feet. The stair ended and the torch showed a flagged floor in front of us. Hugo moved forward enough to enable the rest of us to reach the level area. The air was cool but not cold or damp and smelt slightly musty with a hint of something chemical I couldn't quite place.

As Hugo moved the torch over the floor it revealed a pair of ancient brown boots and I just had time to think this might be no more than a junk room when raising the beam slightly, he revealed a pair of legs clad in breeches, rising from the boots. He swung the beam up to show the full figure of a man arrayed in the garb of a bygone era. To his left breast was attached a name badge with the legend: *Footman, 18th Century*.

'It's a waxwork,' said Hugo, 'presumably one of those formerly on display in the house and for some reason removed.'

At that moment Petronella, who was bringing up the rear behind the two older women, spoke.

'I've found what feels like a light switch. In case it's bright it might be best if we close our eyes before I press it.'

We complied and I could sense light though my closed lids. I opened them slowly but in fact it was quite dim, though bright enough to reveal the former ice cave as an extensive cavity and filled with perhaps nine or ten rows, each containing eight figures, of men and women dressed in clothes of various periods and looking eerily life-like in the gloom. Mrs Miller gasped and I felt a frisson of horror myself. Like the footman each had a name badge, or rather a designation of occupation and an approximate date.

We stood surveying them. On the back wall of the rough-hewn cellar was a large notice, black letters on white background arrogantly proclaiming: Family Servants.

My eyes dropped from it to the figures in the back row and I received a real shock. They seemed all to be young women, although I immediately adjusted that to shop mannequins dressed as women in fashions that could have no conceivable place in any normal household, impractically short micro skirts, plunging and abbreviated tops revealing bare midriffs, legs ending in boots or very high heeled shoes. Their faces were not the bland almost featureless visages of the usual mannequin however, but were realistic and provocatively made up.

'Hugo,' I murmured, and pointed. 'They seem out of place.' We walked to the back and surveyed them from close to. Each girl had one arm thrust forward, the hand turned and fingers arranged to display between thumb and first finger a small placard. The one at the nearer end of the row said: Street walker, Liverpool, 1975. Hugo shone his torch in her face, the better to illumine it. He faced me with a grim expression and spoke in a low voice.

'She isn't a shop dummy; this is a real

woman who's been mummified.' His revelation released a flood of horror through
my mind. Belatedly I recalled that formalin was a constituent of embalming fluid
especially those used for long term preservation of human bodies.

Preoccupied as we were by our observa-
tions, we didn't really notice the others
following us to the back of the ice cave,
but now Mrs Miller emitted a curious cry,
a compound of gasp and scream, followed
by a single word.

'Jim!'

I followed the direction of her gaze to
the further end of the line. The last figure
was not a woman but an elderly man,
dressed in work clothes and with a tool
box between his feet which were set
slightly apart. Hugo and I moved quickly
towards him and examined the badge on
his lapel: *Odd job man, 2005*. Mrs Miller
had started to cry and Petronella was
endeavouring to support and comfort her.
It was obvious that the final mummy in
the row was her former husband.

'I'm very sorry Mrs Miller. If you
recognise this as your husband then we

are far too late to help him,' said Hugo in the gentlest voice I'd ever heard him use. 'All we can do is find out who was responsible and ensure they are brought to justice.'

'Take your aunt outside if you would,' Hugo suggested to the younger woman, 'and it would be best if you went too Aunt Em. It's possible that this room will be deemed a crime scene so we mustn't contaminate it more than we can help.'

Hugo and I remained only long enough to confirm that the remaining figures in the back row were indeed mummified women. Their labels identified them as from various cities in the north west and a cluster of dates in the late nineties, but all were described plainly but brutally it seemed to me as 'street walkers'. There was something familiar about their features and poses and it struck me they were probably used as models for the modern drawings in the art collection. We climbed the stairs and found the women waiting for us at the top.

'Right,' said Hugo. 'Let's get out of this place and find a police station.' An admirable idea which was to be thwarted by the appearance of an individual dressed in obviously expensive country clothes.

'What the devil are you people doing in there?' he demanded in an angry and arrogant voice. 'This area is strictly private — totally off-limits to the hoi-polloi. I alone am permitted to feast my eyes on these lovely odalisques and those inferiors.' As he uttered these words his gaze shifted to the back row of figures and I fancied that his eyes were devouring the mummified girls with ghoulish intensity.

'Are you Lord Cruikscar?' asked Hugo calmly.

'I answer to no-one, certainly not you,' was the furious response. 'And since you don't answer my question you can stay there.' He pulled the door shut with a bang and we heard the padlock being clicked into place.

We all stood silently for a moment or two.

'That's torn it,' said Petronella.

Hugo put his shoulder to the door but

predictably it didn't budge. Apart from anything else he was pushing against the hinges. This observation gave me an idea (I do get them occasionally, though not often enough to propel me to success).

'Shine your torch on the hinges would you Hugo.' He obliged and we could both see there were three of them and although the frame plate of each was buried in the wall, the long arm was held to the back of the door by six large screws apiece. What's more the screws didn't look as though their rust was ancient. I fetched Mr Miller's toolbox and we rooted through it until we found a suitably sized screwdriver. The screws were quite stubborn but Hugo and I took it in turns to work on them, careful not to ruin the heads.

It took a while but eventually we had them all out and could pull the door towards us, leaving it held up only by the padlocked latch on its other side. We were all very relieved to escape that macabre dungeon. The bright sunshine mocked our horror of what we'd seen.

We hastened towards the castle and round to the front. We could hear sirens getting rapidly closer and there was a crowd of people at the end of the drive. We hurried towards them.

'Has something happened?' asked Hugo rather inanely. The woman from the reception desk swung round.

'There's been a terrible accident.'

Just then a police car arrived with an ambulance close behind and another squad car in close pursuit. Confusion followed but to sum up what had happened, pieced together from various accounts and shorn of its drama, Lord Cruikscar in a towering rage had jumped into a sports car and shot off down the drive and through the gate in a high speed right turn and smashed straight into the left side of his mother's Rolls, right where she was sitting. They were both killed instantly. The chauffeur was lucky to escape with a few abrasions and a severe case of shock.

The police quickly took charge, urging people back to allow the ambulance crew to deal with the survivor and victims of the crash. Hugo approached the nearest constable. I didn't hear what he said but I heard the reply.

'Sorry sir, I can't leave here; this is a very serious accident, so if you would be kind enough to leave us to deal with it I'd appreciate it.' Hugo reached into an inside pocket from which he retrieved a small plastic wallet which he opened and passed without comment to the officer who studied it carefully and then returned it.

'Sorry sir, I didn't realise. What is it you want to tell me.'

'We have discovered a number of concealed bodies which I believe to be those of victims of murders carried out over a number of years.'

The constable was clearly taken aback.

'I appreciate,' went on Hugo, 'that you can't leave here immediately but I think you had better radio for backup straight away. There are at least eight bodies which should give someone an idea of the resources which need to be dispatched.'

'Right sir, you'll remain here until they arrive?'

'Of course.'

When the policeman had hurried to one of the patrol cars to contact the station Hugo turned to me.

'It'll obviously be best that I do remain here but I am unhappy at leaving the cave open for anyone to wander in. It is in effect a crime scene. It's clearly impossible to re-secure it for the moment but perhaps you wouldn't mind going back there and keeping an eye on things.' I nodded.

The police response to the constable's plea for aid was commendably prompt and I was not left long in sole custody of that macabre ice house. Soon enough Hugo joined me accompanied by a plainclothes sergeant.

'You don't need more people than necessary down there,' I said. 'I'll wait up here.' The sergeant nodded and he and Hugo descended. They weren't long. The policeman's face was ashen as he re-emerged and I could appreciate how he felt.

'Perhaps you could give me a preliminary statement of how you discovered this,' he said. Hugo and I obliged. Although we kept it as brief as possible it took a while but eventually we were free to rejoin the women. We left him guarding the scene while he awaited the attendance of the crime scene technicians and the medical team. We passed a convoy of vans and ambulances as we walked back along the drive. I asked Hugo about the card he'd flashed at the constable originally.

'It must have been impressive,' I said.

'Oh it was a permit I was given when the Home Office employed me as a consultant in a rather curious matter which entailed me examining a variety of specimens kept in high security areas. This has reminded me I really ought to return it. I just never seem to get time and they haven't reminded me, not recently anyway. Still, lucky I had it with me; speeded things up.' I agreed about that. It was plainly a powerful looking docket. It caused me to view Hugo with rather more respect than had previously been my wont!

There's little more of interest to tell. It seemed obvious that Jim Miller had indeed penetrated the ice cave and was murdered in consequence of his having discovered its secret. He was at last given a quietly decent burial. The police did their best to identify the other victims but with little success. It would appear that most were illegal immigrants trafficked from Eastern Europe and so had never been reported as missing. The undoubted perpetrator of the abductions and murders had been killed in the accident. Lady Cruickscar was certainly an accomplice after the fact for concealing things she must surely have known but since she too was dead the exact extent of her guilt was difficult to gauge. The title of Baron Cruickscar passed to a distant cousin together with the castle and all it contained once the victims and such evidence as there was had been removed.

In the relation of this tale I have altered some of the names due to certain iniquitous aspects of the laws of libel which enable the rich and powerful to suppress, hide and bury the truth by threatening ruin and even imprisonment for anyone revealing it. I struggled with my courage and my conscience over this. Whether I would eventually have been brave enough to challenge those laws and use the real name of Lord Cruikscar I still don't know, as the woman I have called Mrs Miller asked me not to reveal the real names of herself and her husband as she didn't want any notoriety to attach to his memory and her plea as a victim I had no qualms about acceding to, indeed it would have been monstrous to deny her. To ensure their anonymity it became more or less essential to do the same for the perpetrators and so I was not in the end put to the test. I try to draw comfort from the dictum of Camus that 'Fiction is the lie through which we tell the truth', though I prefer to paraphrase it as 'Through fiction's deceits the truth can be told'.

Sometime after these events, Hugo informed me that his Great-Aunt Emily and Mrs Miller had decided that as Aunt Em's house was far too big for her and because Edna Miller could not afford to continue living at the hotel and in any case no longer had any reason to do so, it made sense for them to share Aunt Em's house. It was easily converted into two semi-separate apartments. Since they got on well together they were both gainers, Mrs Miller having otherwise nowhere to live and Great-Aunt Emily benefiting from the companionship and sense of security it brought and which becomes more desirable as one grows older.

This episode, macabre and tragic though it was for so many people, had one potentially positive outcome for me personally. I am now in regular email correspondence with Petronella (not all of it concerning the Science Reference Library!) and we have met on an encouraging number of occasions in both London and Wetherby. I do have a suspicion that Hugo's Great-Aunt Emily's insistence that it would be very helpful if Hugo were to persuade me to assist him in the resolution of this enigma might have had some such outcome in view, but I don't care! I am feeling happier than I have for a very long time.

THE END

We do hope that you have enjoyed reading this large print book.

Did you know that all of our titles are available for purchase?

We publish a wide range of high quality large print books including:
Romances, Mysteries, Classics
General Fiction
Non Fiction and Westerns

Special interest titles available in large print are:
The Little Oxford Dictionary
Music Book, Song Book
Hymn Book, Service Book

Also available from us courtesy of Oxford University Press:
Young Readers' Dictionary
(large print edition)
Young Readers' Thesaurus
(large print edition)

For further information or a free brochure, please contact us at:
Ulverscroft Large Print Books Ltd.,
The Green, Bradgate Road, Anstey,
Leicester, LE7 7FU, England.
Tel: (00 44) **0116 236 4325**
Fax: (00 44) **0116 234 0205**